Blood Orange

By

Brenda M. Spalding

ISBN:069-292737- 9
ISBN: 978-0-692-92737-3

This is a work of fiction

Published by Heritage Publishing U.S.
www.heritagepublishedus.com

To all the brave men and women that

are on the front lines trying to keep

drugs off our streets, from the DEA

agents to the local police officers.

The war on drugs will continue to be

fought and eventually won.

Chapter One

Nora tipped her hat forward above her hazel eyes. The sound of Jasper's hooves echoed throughout the grove as they cantered down the dusty road. Nora Hollister had an affectionate habit of talking to her horse as she rode. "Isn't it a wonderful day, Jasper?" Jasper shook his head in agreement.

Jasper was her ten-year-old Appaloosa gelding—a birthday gift to Nora from her mom and dad when she'd finished college.

Pam and Joe Hollister had been killed three years earlier—on a business trip to Jacksonville in her dad's new Piper Malibu. Engine trouble shortly after takeoff brought the plane down near Lakeland. Riding Jasper seemed to bring her closer to the parents she had lost that day. He was the link.

Nora coveted the quiet of the grove early in the morning and the time it allowed in preparation for the day ahead. Her family had owned this grove and cattle ranch for over a century. The first Hollister had arrived in Florida shortly after the Seminole Wars ended in 1858. Only the bravest had settled in Florida during those turbulent times. The Hollisters owned two hundred and ten acres, divided between an orange grove and a cattle enterprise.

The sun was barely up, and she could already feel the heat of the day rising from the dirt road. Even in early April, the sun could be fierce. Soon the cool sea breeze off the bay would collide with the warmth of the land, and bring the afternoon showers so typical of the Florida summer.

Birds called to each other and sang their intimate songs. Baritone frogs croaked in the pond. Jasper pounded the road, while Nora's leather saddle creaked softly beneath her. A slight breeze rustled the palm trees. The scent of ripe citrus was strong in the balmy air, as the last of the oranges were being picked.

The sun rising in its azure blue and rose-pink colors always made her happy. She pushed her hat back up, and looking to the sky, watched a flock of white ibis glide forth on their way to some watery feeding grounds.

Her grandfather and the farm were all Nora had left of her family and her childhood, and she treasured both. She'd recently implored Gramps to let her take a hand in the running of the day-to-day operations of the farm, but, so far, that request had been repeatedly waved away by the old man.

She had worked hard attaining her MBA, and she desperately wanted to deploy those business skills toward the good of their family legacy, but the cantankerous old gentleman was, at this point, immovable. "Women just don't belong in business," her Gramps would say, every time she brought up the subject. If Gramps didn't relinquish some control soon, she might just seek a job further north, away from the blistering Florida heat, and try to garner some genuine appreciation for her talents.

Frank Hollister, her "Gramps," was fast approaching his eightieth birthday. He had the usual health problems that an eighty-year-old man would have, and it was probably time for him to take it just a touch easier. But he was a stubborn old country codger and was not interested in turning over the business to anyone else.

In addition to the issue regarding managing the business, there was the problem of her grandfather's declining health. Nora was afraid that she could soon find herself her grandfather's caretaker, as opposed to Gramps taking care of her.

It wasn't that she wanted to shirk that responsibility; it was the fact that thinking about it made her a little sad and nostalgic for her childhood. And what about the inevitable, her grandfather's death? A life without her grandfather was really depressing to think about. It was during times like these that Nora most missed her parents' guidance.

Later that morning, Nora rode Jasper to the packing house with Gramps' lunch. Lunch time was still two hours away, but it would be too hot then for a ride, so it had to be now. Rosita, their housekeeper and cook, had found Gramps' lunch on the counter by the back door, left behind. It had become increasingly apparent that Gramps was getting more forgetful these days. Cajoling him into seeing a doctor for anything was never easy, but this was a reminder for Nora that she had to try again.

Nora rounded a corner, and the packing house came into view. It was a squat, green, metal and cinder block building, situated in the middle of the grove. Unassuming as it was, it represented central operations headquarters in terms of running the Hollister Farm. As a child, the packing house had been her very own playground, and the workers and their families on the farm were her friends. It was nearing the end of the picking season. Soon the workers would move on as the sweltering days of summer began.

The migrant workers, most of whom started laboring before sunrise, dropped off their early loads of oranges, and then usually hung around the packing house for a while. To say it is hard labor picking oranges doesn't do the task justice, as almost a hundred percent of all picking was still done by hand.

The pickers would climb a ladder with an empty sack slung over their shoulder—with each sack eventually holding about two hundred of whatever citrus they were assigned to pick that day. First to ripen were the grapefruit, followed by different varieties of oranges.

Flatbed trailers carried empty tubs into the grove, with each tub expecting a capacity of 900 pounds of ripe fruit. A special truck called a *goat* would hoist the filled tubs with a hydraulic boom and drive them back to the packing house for sorting. The fruit would then be conveyed to factories, where it was destined to be made into juice, or sold to distributers for sale at grocery stores. Agents did all the deal-making in air-conditioned Tampa and seldom came to the sweltering groves in Myakka or Arcadia.

The workers dutifully checked in with their supervisor, Tito Ramirez, at the packing house. He was not well liked by the workers. Tito was short and thin, but what he lacked in size, he made up in sheer, unadulterated attitude. His family was originally from Cuba, and had settled in Ybor City after finding work in the cigar factories there.

He didn't like factory work, where he had been continually ordered around. In the Hollister packing plant, however, he was *El Jefe*, the boss, calling his own shots, ordering the others around. He'd been with the farm for four years and had become even more difficult to work with this year—his arrogance growing. He was abrupt and surly with the workers and assumed a superior attitude toward them, which the workers chafed at.

Nora coaxed Jasper into the packing house yard, just as Gramps was talking to Tito in the packing bay. If she was any judge of body language, an argument was in progress. Both parties appeared quite agitated about something.

Dismounting, she tied Jasper to a ring set into the wall just for him, and then—bolting the seven stairs to the loading platform—she left Jasper to slake his thirst in the watering trough. She approached the two men cautiously, and listened.

"I don't care what those stupid migrants say. Do they even know how to count? I can, and I'm good at it. Who are you going to believe, me or them?" Tito spat out.

"Now listen here, Tito. I expect that the ticket book is going to match up every day. If I hear any more complaints, I'm going to do more than just talk to you. You understand me? I'll not have these workers cheated! They work long and hard just to make the money they do, which isn't a lot, but whatever it is, they need all of it," Gramps said angrily, his voice rising.

"Do what you will." Tito turned, raising his arms, dismissing the conversation as he stormed away, mumbling to himself.

Nora closed the distance, asking, "Gramps, what was that all about?"

"Our workers complain that Tito is not giving them proper credit for all the fruit they collect. They think he's a cheat," Gramps thundered, as he turned to go back to his office.

"How does he get off treating them like that? They deserve to get paid for *all* the work they do. We've built a good reputation here, and that's why these workers have returned to *us,* year-after-year, for generations! Gosh, they've raised their children in our groves!" Nora interjected, her indignation growing. She felt a heightened flush on her face—and not from the Florida heat. She'd grown up playing with some of these workers as a child, and enjoyed traditional meals with them. They were like family to her. She would not tolerate them being cheated, or abused.

"I understand, sweetheart, but we have to find a way to prove it. Tito is the only one checking them in. He had a fit when I suggested that someone assist him with the ticket book. I really do believe that something is going on."

He carried on talking while walking to his office, his old dog Rex right on his heels, "Too many complaints from different workers for there not to be something to it." Gramps sat behind his cluttered desk. He shuffled and tossed a few things aside. "I'm getting too old for this."

Nora stood before him with her hands on her hips. "Gramps, this is why I went to college and got a business degree. Please let me help you. I can do a lot of this paper work, talking to the agents and other things for you. It's been four years since I graduated, and you won't let me do more than order equipment and talk to the Department of Agriculture. I want more to do. I need more to do. My degree is being wasted."

Nora paced up and down in the small room, working up another good head of steam. Besides the fact that she did want more to do, she also knew her Gramps was wearing out. She was afraid for his health, and she had to find a way to convince him to let her help.

"You're right. I promise next season you can take over this office. I'll step down a bit."

"You say that every year, but it never happens. The start of picking season next year will be the same as this one. Gramps, if I can't work here, I'll have to find a job in another grove, or quit the business altogether."

"I'm sorry, Nora," Gramps said, standing up, and motioning for her to stop her pacing. Suddenly, he grabbed her shoulders, and looked into her eyes. She looked so much like her mother, Pam, with the same chestnut hair and deep brown eyes. She also had her mother's willful spirit. His son had made a great choice when he had taken Pam as his wife.

Releasing his grip on the startled Nora, he said, "I tell you what. You come in here tomorrow, and you can start by helping to organize this office. The end of the season is coming. The office will be yours next year, and I'll only be here if you have questions. I had planned on passing the operation over to your father, but that can't happen, and it's time for you to take charge."

Nora read between the lines and knew what the old man meant. She was still a girl to him. If she had been born male, this moment would have happened before this. Her Gramps was a wonderful man, but it was 1986, and he was still stuck in the 1950's, she thought.

"You'd better mean it this time, because I mean it. I work, or I'm gone."

"I meant it, too. It will give me some time to deal with Tito," Gramps said.

Nora pointed out the paper bag with his lunch. "Rosita said you forgot your lunch again. Can we please have the doctor give you a once-over?"

"I don't want that old quack poking around my insides when I feel fine. I've got a lot on my mind, is all," Gramps fired back.

"Ok, how about doing it for me?" Nora took the old man by the shoulders, just as he had done with her a moment ago, and looked him in the eyes. "You're all I've got, and I'm afraid to lose you. Please, Gramps. Just to make sure nothing is brewing inside you that we need to take care of," she touched his chest, and gave him a look that she hoped would make him cave in.

"Sure, okay," he said reluctantly, and gave in as she prayed he would. "You call the quack and set it up."

Nora gave Gramps a hug and batted him on the shoulder, "I'll call tomorrow."

As she was riding home, it dawned on her that Gramps missed her dad as much as she did. He was holding on, working, afraid to recognize that his son would not be taking over the business. She felt sorry for the older man and for herself. They were both still grieving in their own way.

Chapter Two

Rosita was surprised to find Nora already at the kitchen table when she arrived the next morning.

"What got you out of bed before the chickens this morning?" she asked—lifting the coffee pot, surprised that it was already made. Rosita spoke with a heavy Spanish accent. Even after nearly thirty years in the States she still spoke with the thick, yet, lyrical tones of her small ciudad natal in Columbia.

"Are you trying to take my job from me?" She lifted the pot and with a curious smile, turned to Nora.

"No, I just couldn't sleep," Nora yawned. "Gramps *actually* said I can start working in his office, finally. He even agreed to let me make an appointment for him with Doc Winters. I should count my blessings, but now he's got me worried something might really be wrong with him, and he's just not telling me. I feel like he may be hiding something from me."

Rosita leaned her ample backside against the counter as she spoke. Nearing her autumn years, she remained a beautiful woman. Her raven-black hair was now streaked with gray, and braided in a precise coil crowning her head. Long golden earrings decorously flanked a nearly wrinkle-free face. She continued to wear the traditional long colorful skirts and peasant blouses of her Columbian heritage.

"I've been working for him since before your parents were married thirty years ago. I have yet to figure him out. Hector and I came to this farm about the same time. We were married in that little chapel out in the grove. We raised our children *and* our grandchildren together, and that man still keeps secrets from us. He is like a fortress, no entrance without the proper words."

Rosita poured a cup of coffee for herself and settled down at the table beside Nora. Placing her hand over Nora's she said, "Don't you worry, mi pequeña. When he is ready, he will tell us. He may just be feeling the weight of his destiny. It comes to us all, one day."

Standing, she opened the cupboard and grabbed a can of cat food for the dark tabby that was winding his way around her legs crying for his breakfast. "Gato, I will be glad when you can open your own cans," she laughed.

Everyone loved that big cat. He'd arrived on their doorstep in the middle of a torrential summer downpour as a young kitten—just fur and bones—and decided to stay. Nora named him Hobo, and their dog Rex instantly accepted him as a new friend.

Hearing Gramps coming down the stairs, they quickly changed the conversation.

"How many more weeks until the picking is done?" Nora inquired.

Shuffling arthritically into the kitchen, while stuffing his shirt into his pants, he responded, "I think two, at the most. Then we can concentrate on the cattle. I'm thinking of getting a new bull, to strengthen the line a bit. Zeus is still, well, strong as a bull, but he's getting older, like me," Gramps grinned. "I'll make some calls, shake the trees, and find out how much a healthy stud is going for now."

"Gramps, remember, you promised I would start taking over some office duties. How about letting me make those calls? You tell me who to call, and coach me what to ask. Please Gramps, I want to learn. I need to feel useful."

"Oh, alright, sure, the file is in the packing house office. Maybe I should start showing you how to run this place. After all, it will all be yours someday." He fixed a battered fedora on his head, and grabbing his lunch sack, left for another long day.

"Madre Dios," Rosita declared. "I see what you mean. He didn't push back like always."

"That's what I'm saying. He should have fought me, made *some* excuse, put me off, but nothing. I'll call Doc Winter at lunch and make that appointment. I don't know, maybe I just finally got through to him. I'm not sure what to think, arrrrgh!" Nora stood, kissed the top of Rosita's head and raced out the door.

She bounded down the steps, two at a time, just as Gramps was pulling the jeep around in the yard. Chickens scattered everywhere. "Wait for me," she called after him.

Gramps stopped the jeep in a cloud of dust. "Come on, then," he said slapping the seat beside him. As she opened the door, Rex, a royal mongrel of indeterminate breed, jumped in front of her, and into the back seat.

"Oh no," Nora said trying to coax the dog out.

"Let him be, Nora," Gramps said gently. "He just wants to go for the ride. He'll wander back on home in a bit."

They rode to the packing house in awkward silence. Nora was bewildered. Gramps had acquiesced to sharing duties and agreed to go to the doctor, but somehow she was more concerned about what was *really* going on with him.

A ruckus had developed in the area where the crews dropped off their loads. Several workers had surrounded Tito and were crowding him in an aggressive manner.

Nora jumped out of the jeep as it still rolled, and ran to insert herself between them.
"Stop this now," she barked. "What's the problem here?"

A worker named Rita shouted, "He's still not giving us a correct count."

"You can't count, you ignorant bitch," Tito hollered back. Nora, sandwiched between them, struggled to hold them apart as Rita took a wild swing at Tito, just over Nora's shoulder.

"Rita is right. He's been cheating us all season," Javier, Rita's husband, exclaimed. Shouts and yells from the gathering crowd all affirmed that they, too, thought Tito was cheating them.

"We are all agreed. Either he gets our counts right, or we all move on to some other job," Javier had started to simmer down, but was still livid. "We've all lost money since coming here. If he is here next season, I swear, we will not be, not a one of us!"

"Tito, in the office," Nora said firmly, hoping to defuse the stand-off.

"I don't listen to you," Tito snarled, showing her his back. "You are not my boss."

"Wrong, Tito! As of this very moment, Nora is your boss," Gramps made his declaration while pacing across the raised platform. "Listen up, everyone, please!" he shouted, facing his loyal workers. "Nora is, from now on, in charge of all operations at this packing house.

"Tito, we *will* find out if you've been cheating, or if you just can't count." Gramps removed his hat, pulled a wrinkled red bandana from a pocket in his overalls, and mopped the sweat off his reddened face.

Nora was stunned. Rita looked at her and shrugged an intimate smile. She was as pleasantly surprised as Nora. The pack of workers turned away and whispered among themselves—confused.

"Tito, you go with Nora as she asked, please. I'll be with you both in a minute," Gramps directed. "Javier, walk with me."

Nora and Tito entered the back office, the tension palpable. Nora, assuming Gramps' reign, took her place behind the big desk, settling decisively in the worn leather armchair that had represented her grandfather's seat of power since she was a child. The fit was perfect, she thought.

Tito sat heavily in a chair across from her, stretching out his small frame to lounge, splayed out in the chair. His condescending body language was silently shouting that he didn't give a crap what she had to say.

"Guess you're going to believe the pickers," he began. "I bet half of 'em are illegal. How about I call INS and have their papers checked?"

Nora startled him by firing back. "Don't threaten me, Tito. You best pray I don't call the police, and have you investigated for theft."

"Theft? Are you crazy, girl?" Tito shot up straight from the rickety chair. "I'm not stealing from nobody. And if the count is off once in a while, just who am I stealing from?" Nervous sweat beaded on his face as he blustered, suggesting his dirty dealing. Tito was digging a hole for himself and didn't even know it.

"You're stealing from the workers," she insisted. "They deserve to be paid in total for the back-breaking work they do. If you put money in your pocket that rightfully belongs to them, you are stealing." Nora was astounded that Tito assumed his oily actions would be tolerated.

"You can't be serious." Tito realized his mistake much too late, and now tried to bluff his way out of it.

"I'm deadly serious," Nora said moving to the front of the desk. Bracing her back against it, she locked her hands firmly before her, challenging him. "You tally the next count right, or you are out of here, for good. The ticket book and the tally sheets must always match, to the nickel, *the nickel*."

Standing nearly toe-to-toe with Nora, trying to intimidate her, Tito bullied, "If you were a man, I'd have to knock you out."

"If you were a real man, we wouldn't be having this conversation."

"Merida," he muttered, shouldering past her, and leaving the office.

Gramps came in as Tito stamped out, "Guess that went well?"

"He *is* up to something with the counts. He almost admitted it." Nora perched herself at the edge of the desk to let Gramps assume his post. "What did you and Javier talk about?"

"I'm going to give Tito just enough rope to hang himself. He thinks he's so damn cunning. I've asked Javier to quietly count all the loads before they even leave the grove. At the end of the week, I'll compare what he has, and what Tito has entered in the books. When, and if, they don't match, we'll have our answer. I'll summon the sheriff while Tito is still here with his hands in the cookie jar. I won't have him running off to cheat someone else."

"Sounds like a masterful plan," Nora smiled appreciatively, slipping off the edge of the desk. "Now, you want to give me something to do? Let me make some of those phone calls for you, maybe round us up a healthy young bull. I'm acquainted with some of the stud ranches out near Arcadia.

Gramps drew open a rusting file drawer, and began rummaging for his notes.

Nora, grabbing a phone and phonebook, practically skipped across the office to clear a place for her to work. The tiny space she'd begun to arrange just the way she liked it, felt like the start of something big for her—momentum. She was finally planting her own flag, on her own Everest. Turning back toward her grandfather, she queried. "Now, who do I call for cattle prices?"

Gramps snickered, "I guess you still need me for something," as he offered her a dog-eared spiral notebook. "Look under cattle brokers. Most ranches are listed by county. Try to find something close by that we can both go look at."

Chapter Three

Nora was increasingly proud of herself as she assumed more control of the company. She'd spent the last week organizing her new office space and preparing for the hard tasks ahead. She found an old slate-top school master's desk, a slightly dented and somewhat rusted filing cabinet to match Gramps', and a tall oak bookcase—crowned with tarnished brass gargoyle bookends. She was amazed at what one could find in the Salvation Army thrift shop in town.

Dusting away the cobwebs and watching for spiders, she paused to laugh at herself. She might be a genuine country girl, but creepy crawlies still scared her like city folk. She made files for the cabinet, compiled her own phone directory, and created a checklist for what she needed to do.

"Gramps, remember we have your doctor's appointment on Monday. We best leave here at noon sharp, to make it to Arcadia on time. If you're a good patient, I'll buy you a black-cherry walnut ice cream cone," she said, as a joke, but was in fact, trying to gauge his reaction.

"I'll remember," he muttered into his shirt. "I wrote it down in my calendar. Now," he sighed, "we have to look at the two counts and see if there is any difference between Tito and Javier. I hope I regret saying this, but I'm betting there will be a substantial difference. I'm not looking forward to any confrontation."

"It will be fine, either way. We need to find out what's really going on and try to get to the bottom of this mess between Tito and the workers," Nora responded.

"O.K., let's go then and get it over with," Gramps said, struggling to his feet. He saw Nora watching him, concerned. "Don't pity me, Nora," he huffed.

"Pity? I didn't say a word."

"Your face sure did. I'm just stiff from sitting too long," he insisted, walking torturously from the small office and toward the packing floor.

"We'll see what the doctor has to say about it Monday," Nora murmured, not loud enough that he could hear her, and then, following him through the door thought, "God forbid, he admits he might have a bit of arthritis at his age."

"Tito," Gramps called out, "Please bring me the count for the week."

"What do you want that for?" Tito asked, challenging him. "I already sent it to payroll."

"I called payroll and told them to hold it for me," Gramps said, anticipating the argument to come."I want to see your tally sheets for each specific day. *Now,* Tito."

"I thought Nora was in charge? Shouldn't I be giving them to her?" he questioned sarcastically.

"Okay Tito, I can play that game," Nora said heatedly. "Give the tally sheets to my grandfather *now.* That is an order from your new boss."

Tito glared at her. He despised taking orders, and even more so, despised taking them from a woman. The tally sheets and ticket books were on a stand-up desk at the front of the loading bay. Tito strode over, and clutching the papers, shoved them defiantly at the older man, "Here, this is everything, just as I have always done them. I do know how to count, you know. And I don't like being treated as a child," he spat, aware that several of the workers were gathered whispering on the platform, and on the ground below. Tito, his nervous guilt getting the best of him, squinted over his shoulder at the group shuffling around behind him, his eyes shifting side to side, as if preparing an escape route.

Gramps, reaching into his back pocket, produced the tally Javier had taken of all the baskets while still in the grove, before the oranges were transported to the packing house.

Shaking his head, Tito stared at his shoes, knowing his numbers were fictitious. He knew he'd been had, and his mind scrambled, trying to come up with any excuse that might save his skin.

"I've had someone checking the loads in the fields, *before* they came back to the packing house," Gramps announced—as if all the workers didn't already know.

He studied both sets of tally sheets, as Tito tried to sneak off the floor, blocked by a few male workers. He'd witnessed the local sheriff exit his patrol car after it had pulled into the yard, and that man was now walking toward the crowd.

"Tito, when I went to school, 2+2 still equaled four, and I'm pretty damn sure you need glasses as well. Mister, I can count!" Gramps exclaimed. "Every day, you are under-counting different workers—a load here, a load there. By my simple reckoning, you've scammed us a hundred loads this week alone. More so, you were warned about short-counting these workers. How stupid and greedy can you be?"

The few workers who had cut off Tito's escape grabbed him roughly by the arms. "We can take care of him, Mr. Hollister," one promised. Some in the crowd had ax handles, and one carried a make-shift noose.

Tito was terrified, "You cannot turn me over to them, Mr. Hollister, please, they will kill me," Tito implored, begging for his life. Gone was the coarse bravado he'd shown moments before.

"Sorry, Mr. Hollister," a tall and unyielding county sheriff interjected, prying Tito from the arms of his would-be tormentors. "I'll take him from here." In one adroit motion, he spun Tito around, and after forcing his hands behind his back, unceremoniously slapped handcuffs on his shaking wrists, ratcheting them tight in humiliation. "I'm sure he will enjoy some 'quality time' in the county jail waiting for the judge to finish his monthly rounds."

One of the men, a big Mexican named Octavio, spoke up, "No judge for this one. We shall be judge, jury and *Verdugo* for the dog that cheats his own kind. We make our own justice in the fields."

"I can't let you do that, as much as I'd like to," the sheriff instructed the men—resting his palm on the handle of the .44 holstered at his side to emphasize his point.

The workers reluctantly let the sheriff take over and do his job. Of course, they'd had other, more permanent plans for Tito, and they grumbled bitterly as they slowly backed off.

"Nice to meet you, Mr. Hollister," the sheriff said politely. "Miss Hollister," he said, nodding a greeting while tipping his hat to Nora, "I'm Sheriff Gabe McAlister. I took over for Sheriff Grady after he retired last month."

"Nice to meet you . . . too," Nora stumbled like a shy school girl over her words. The sheriff was a ruggedly handsome man, *and* well mannered, no doubt about it.

"Well, I'd better get this guy back." He raised his Stetson with one hand and held onto Tito with the other. "You, get." He pulled Tito toward his patrol car, and not too gently, forced him into the back seat.

Nora watched him get into the driver's seat and pull out of the yard. She stood, hands in her pockets, thinking, "My, my things are suddenly a tad more interesting around here."

Chapter Four

The following Sunday morning saw the sun rising in clouds of purple and pink, promising a perfect day ahead. A stiff west breeze stirred the sandy ground—creating dust-devils that danced like dervishes among the devout families who were gathering in celebration for an early Mass.

Father Miguel Lopez arrived promptly at 7:00 a.m. to begin Catholic services for his flock, most of whom were field workers.

Nora's great-grandfather had built a small wooden chapel on the grounds near the worker's compound. Rosita and Hector had been married there, along with countless other couples over the decades. Sky-blue shutters fixed to cast-iron hinges on the outside window frames could be opened or closed, according to the day's weather. Today, they were open on all sides to let the morning's refreshingly cool breeze flow through.

Ancient, old-growth oak trees towered over benches and picnic tables hand-hewn in place by Nora's great-grandfather to provide an oasis shaded from the sun. Families gathered in this treasured shade to talk of things other than hard work, and to care for their beloved children as they played. Sunday was always a day off on the Hollister Farm. Not all commercial groves honored this, the Lord's Day.

Nora and Gramps arrived just as Father Miguel was beginning the Mass. The good padre traveled between several groves—often over great distance—serving the mostly Catholic migrant workers to baptize a newborn infant or perform the marriage of a young couple, sometimes both on the same day.

On these special occasions, the other workers would organize a small fiesta to celebrate. Rainbow-colored lantern lights would be festooned upon the grand old oaks, and an entire pig or cow would be barbecued over a large open pit in the ground. Guitars and *bajo sexton* would appear, played by the elderly men who could no longer work the fields. The joyous sounds of music and dancing would fill the air, and for a while, clichés notwithstanding, all troubles could disappear in that magical moment.

Nora found the Latin liturgy of the Mass soothing. During the reading of the gospel, her mind wandered off subject to the new sheriff's startling blue eyes and thick black hair. She recalled him standing there—tall, dark and handsome. He had a small scar running from the corner of his left eye to his hairline. She wondered where he had gotten it. Was he still a boy then? Was he injured doing something heroic?

Gramps liked to shake hands with the workers as they left chapel to show appreciation for their loyalty and hard work. He stood beside the priest and greeted the workers as they filed past, smiling and addressing them by name.

Hector Sanchez, Rosita's husband, stopped to talk to his employer. "Pardon for me, Mr. Hollister," he began, twisting a well-worn straw hat in his hands. "May I ask who will be doing the counting in the packing house now that Tito is gone?"

"I thought I might offer you the job," Gramps said. "You know the workers best, and they respect you. You already work well with the cattle, but they shouldn't take so much of your time that you cannot assume this important duty, a duty of trust.

Let me know tomorrow morning if you've decided to accept it, or not. There will be a small raise in it for you." After some parting words, the men firmly shook hands, leaving Hector to run and catch up to his anxious wife.

"Who did he choose?" Rosita begged—her curiosity palpable. Of course, she'd been the one who prompted him to ask in the first place.

"He said that the job was mine if I wanted it. Ay, a big decision," Hector mused, twisting his hat while alternately running his fingers restlessly through his salt-and-pepper hair.

"What's to think about? Of course, you want it! You better think fast," Rosita said slyly. "I don't think your hat will last, if you take too long."

"Very funny," he returned, slapping his hat on his head. Arms linked in spousal confidence, they strolled among the venerable trees, greeting friends as they made their way to the little home reserved just for them. Since they were permanent staff, and not migrant, their house was bigger and had been maintained better than the others. Rosita had planted fragrant flowers in a box Hector had built for her, and mounted under the front window so their perfume could waft into the small living room on warm evenings. He had broken and tilled a small plot of ground behind their home where

Rosita cultivated a small vegetable garden. Tomatoes and zucchini were her favorites. These vegetables, her labor of love, often found their way to the Hollister table.

Nora, after talking with many of the workers, joined Gramps and Father Miguel.

"The workers want to find out who is going to replace Tito," she inquired.

"I told Hector he can have the job, if he wants it. He's a hard worker and admired by the workers," Gramps added.

A billowing red cloud of dust advanced—cloaking the road and catching Nora's attention. "I wonder who that could be," Nora said, pointing her chin in the direction of a sheriff's patrol car approaching—as her heart skipped like a school-girl waiting for a prom invitation. She wanted it to be Gabe McAlister, but at the same time, in contradiction to herself, hoped it wasn't.

"Well, hello again, Sheriff," Gramps called out as the car came to a halt.

Gabe, with surprising agility for a six-footer, quickly jumped out of the cruiser and—donning a pair of reflective sunglasses—called out, "Hello, Mr. Hollister, Nora, Father."

"Gabe, I'd like you to meet Father Miguel Lopez. He comes to say the mass for the workers on Sundays," Gramps said introducing the two.

"Pleased to meet you, Father. I'm sure the workers appreciate your traveling to them," Gabe offered—firmly shaking the shorter priest's outstretched hand.

The old priest looked at Gabe and Nora—smiling. He had a funny feeling that these two might need his services in the not too distant future. Removing the purple silk ceremonial stole from around his neck, along with the white cotton surplice in which he'd said the Mass, he answered, "Thank you, my son. Sorry I cannot stay to talk. I have other groves to visit before it gets too hot. This black cassock is not designed for the highest sun," he said pulling at the floor-length garment.

Father Miguel left them and climbed into a derelict, early-sixties Pontiac Catalina sedan. There was no way anyone could tell what color it originally had been. Most of the paint had worn off, bleached by the sun, and someone had used their finger to write "baptize me" in the dust obscuring the back window.

Gabe returned his attention to Nora and her grandfather. "I thought I'd drop by and give you guys an update on the Tito situation."

"I hope you threw away the key to his cell," Nora snarled, unable to suppress her anger at what Tito had clearly done to cheat his own crew.

"Not exactly," Gabe answered her sourly. "We had him in a cell with another guy who was up on drug charges. The two idiots got to talking, and some yahoo bailed them both out just before midnight."

"Do you know who posted his bail?" Nora demanded. "I can't believe that dirty coyote got out."

"His bail was not set very high, just three thousand, and with a good bail bondsman, that's only three hundred dollars. I suspect the other man, Richie Cantura, had a bit to do with helping him make bail. I'm having one of my men try to trace it back. The thing is: you don't get any favors from Cantura without having to pay it back, in spades. If not with money, then you work it off.

"Richie is in with some pretty bad people. We caught him peddling cocaine, and hoped we could put him away for a long while. Now he's out, I don't expect we'll see him anytime soon."

"So, if I hear you right, this guy Richie is in with a group of drug dealers. Now they may have Tito working for them, too?" Nora asked.

"It may be worse than that. Rumor says Richie is a small fish in one of the big drug cartels. I've been getting some information off the streets. I'm not sure how reliable it is, though."

Gramps had been listening, "A drug cartel? Really—up here in Myakka? I thought they were mostly down in Miami, not up here."

"Sir, they are spreading all over Florida. The smuggling of drugs into this country is getting worse every year. This cartel is organized from Columbia and is the worst of the lot."

Gabe was silent for a moment. "Nora, be careful if Tito shows up around here. He should head straight for Ybor City and his family, if he's smart. Unfortunately, I doubt he is."

Nora offered her hand to Gabe. "Thanks for coming by, Sheriff. We'll call you if he shows up."

Gabe took her hand and held it longer than usual for a casual moment. Their eyes locked. Nora broke first. "Well, goodbye, Sheriff. Come by anytime." She walked over to his patrol car with him. They stood there facing each other like statues, and just as silent.

"Nora, Rosita will be waiting for us back at the house," Gramps said, breaking the spell. Nora and Gramps climbed into the old jeep, and roaring away, headed for the house and Rosita's waiting breakfast.

Gabe got back inside his car, reflexively turned the key and started the engine and drove away distracted.

Chapter Five

Doctor Winter's office was in his house—a rambling, older Victorian style with a wraparound porch. The waiting room was also the reception room. It was in the original dining room. Dark wood wainscoting covered the lower half of the walls. Faded wallpaper that was decades out of date took over the top half. Doc's exam room was across the hall in what used to be the sitting room.

"Frank, about time Nora got you in here," Doctor Winters said, scolding Gramps. "At your age, you can't leave things to chance. Sit up on the table, and we'll give you a once-over." Doc was in his sixties and had been around for most of the births and deaths in the area. He was an old-time general practitioner.

"Doc, this is a waste of your time and mine," Gramps said—struggling a bit to climb up on the exam table. The only staff was a receptionist who was also his nurse. Nurse Clara Hill was a crusty woman in her fifties. She had retired from the Army Medical Corps and had a drill sergeant attitude toward the patients. But they all knew that underneath her gruff exterior was a heart of gold.

"Not a waste of my time. I get paid for taking care of you," Doc pulled the stethoscope out of his pocket and put it around his neck.

"Unbutton a couple of your shirt buttons, and I'll have a listen. Nora tells me that you are forgetting things a bit lately."

"Nora is a worry wart."

"Maybe, maybe not," Doc said putting the stethoscope to Gramps' chest. "Take a deep breath—and again." He moved around the table to reach behind his patient. "Take a breath and hold it." Judging by the look on his face, he was not happy with what he was hearing.

"Frank, your lungs are not functioning as good as they should, and I heard a bit of a murmur in there. You're not a spring chicken anymore. You need to take it a bit easier. Cut back on the hours at the Grove."

"Ah, you worry too much, just like Nora," declared the old man.

"Look, Frank, I'm here if you want to talk. We can go into the kitchen. Clara always has the coffee on. We can just talk like old friends. You do understand I'm your friend, as well as your doctor."

"Maybe another time. I've got things to do," Gramps said.

"Level with me. Are you feeling okay? Is something bothering you?"

"The only thing bothering me is people worrying about me." Gramps took a breath and made a decision. "I give up. You want to hear what's bothering me? I'm worried about what is gonna happen to the grove when I'm gone. If Joe had lived, I'd have it planned out already. God, I miss my son. I love Nora, don't misunderstand me, but I want my son back. I want Joe back. I want what should have been." A tear escaped and ran down the old man's cheek. He swiped at it with a hand that had seen years of hard work. He was embarrassed that Doc had seen him crying.

"Aw, Frank," Doc placed a hand on his shoulder. "I understand. Remember I lost my brother, Donald, in Viet Nam—right at the end of the war. We were going to set up practice together. I think of him most every day. But what's wrong with

Nora?" Doc queried softly. "She has a degree in agriculture and another in business management."

"Nora is great, but she's a female. She'll get married and have kids. Maybe move away. I'll be left with the farm and no one to give it to."

"Frank, women work now, just like men. They raise families and still have great jobs. Look at Nurse Hill. She was in the army, for Pete's sake. She was in Viet Nam serving her country and now she's working here. Did you know she has three grown children and seven grandchildren? Talk to Nora about what she wants to do. She just might surprise you."

Gramps buttoned his shirt and made his way off the exam table. "I guess you're right. But what if she learns the business and then walks away?"

"If Nora has anything to say about it, she will leave only if you chase her away. Think about it."

They walked out together to see Nurse Hill. "Clara, I would like you to make an appointment for Frank here. He needs some tests done at Manatee Memorial.

"Whoa. You never said anything about tests," Gramps protested.

"Don't work yourself up about it. Just some routine things, a blood test to start. I want to check out your heart and lungs, but I can't do those things here. It will take a single day out of your busy schedule. Frank, you're over seventy. Time to make sure that everything under the hood is in running condition."

Nora came in the door to pick up her crotchety ol' gramps. She could tell by the look on his face that he was not happy. "Well, how did it go?" she asked both men.

"Basically, he's fine, but I'm sending him to Manatee Memorial for some routine tests. Nurse Hill will give you a call once everything is set up," said Doc Winters.

"I don't see what the big deal is," Gramps said. "I'm getting old and forgetting stuff, so what?" He was still spoiling for a fight, but Nora could tell it was all bluff.

"Don't worry, Doc. You get him signed up, and I'll get him there." Even if I have to hog tie him and drag him there, she thought.

Nurse Hill called the next patient as Nora and Gramps walked out to the car. Gramps stuck his hand out for the car keys. "I'm not senile yet. I remember how to drive, and I can still find the way home."

Nora turned over the keys, not looking forward to what would probably be a silent ride home.

Gramps pulled out of the parking lot and headed away from home towards downtown Arcadia.

"Ah, you're heading the wrong way," Nora cringed.

"You promised me an ice cream cone if I went to that old quack. I did, so you owe me."

Nora chuckled at the old man, "You're right. I almost forgot. Henry's on the corner has the best black raspberry. What are you going to have?"

"Coffee, dipped in chocolate, and I can't wait."

The sun was setting when they pulled back into the yard. Poor old Rex walked slowly down the steps to greet them. His tail wagged so hard his whole body shook.

"Come on, old thing," Gramps said. "Pretty soon they'll be putting both of us out to pasture. I'll get you some dinner, and then I'll tell you all about that darn Doc Winters and what he's doing to me." The last bit he said for Nora's benefit.

Nora was beat. She didn't need any supper after the double scoop of black raspberry ice cream. Gramps fed his dog, turned on the television, sat back in his recliner and was asleep with Rex by his feet in no time.

It was still early, not yet eight o'clock. Nora fixed herself a glass of iced tea and went out to sit on the back porch. She loved this time of year. The nights were still cool enough to sit out. A couple of years ago she had convinced her grandfather to screen-in the porch. Without it, the mosquitoes were terrible and could ruin a nice evening like this.

She sat back in an ancient rocker, sipping her tea and watching some bats as they swooped by, catching their dinner. She reached for the book she'd been reading, pulled the chain on the lamp beside her and looked forward to a relaxing evening. Her old cat, Hobo, hopped on her lap and after several turns settled down to nap.

A brand new black Ford E-250 van stopped at the back gate to the old ranch next to the Hollister place. The gate had a big lock and chain holding it shut.

Richie and Tito were inside the van, with another guy called "Santos." Neither of the two men knew him, or whether that was his real name. They only knew he was the one running the operation tonight. He was tall and dark, with a slight build, and he was covered with prison tats. The vibe coming off him was scary, and they both knew he was not a person to be fooled with. His English was excellent, but his slight accent placed him as coming from South America. Richie thought Santos might be from Columbia, and told Tito to be very careful around him.

"Take that bolt cutter, Richie, and cut that lock off," Santos demanded.

"Why do I have to do it?"

"Shit, just do it," Santos replied sternly, indicating he didn't like his orders being questioned, not even a little. Richie grumbled, but did as he was told, slamming the van door on the way out. Both men cringed at the sound.

"Is he loco?" grumbled Santos.

"Probably," said Tito. He hoped no one had heard the door slam. Old man Jessup was hard of hearing, but not deaf. Richie did as he was told. The lock pinged as the hasp was cut. He tossed the lock and chain into the tall grass by the fence and walked back to the van, opening the door to get back in, but Santos stopped him.

"Are we going to drive through closed gates, estúpido?" Santos asked, shaking his head. "And don't slam the door this time." He shook his head again in disbelief.

Richie made a face behind his back, and closed the door softly. He walked in front of the van again and opened the gates. The van pulled through, and he hopped back in.

They drove the van around to the side of the house where it faced the big pasture. "Get out and take a look around, and be quiet about it," Santos directed.

Tito and Richie each went around the house. Santos stayed off to the side of the house watching the door and the pasture.

Henry Jessup was not sleeping well that night. He'd been fighting a cold that had gotten the better of him and was up late watching television. He sensed something, not sure what exactly, and got his shotgun from the closet by the porch door. He checked to make sure it was loaded, grabbed a flashlight, and walked out onto the porch.

He stopped, turned up his hearing aid and tried to listen for unusual sounds. His cattle were nervous and moving around in the back field. Something had them stirred up. He figured it might be a bobcat looking for a meal. He had a couple of calves out there that would be an easy target if one came calling.

The screen door squeaked as he pushed it open. He heard something again, that's for sure. "Shit," he exclaimed in a whisper. He walked down the wooden steps, and intentionally made some noise. "Okay, cat, you better leave my cattle alone." He swung the light around, heading for the back pasture. He completely froze as he suddenly felt the pressure of a gun to his head.

"No *gato*, old man, but I can sure move like one," Santos said, slowly taking the shotgun from the old man's hands, as well as the flashlight.

"What the hell do you think you're doing? This is my land," Henry said.

"We don't want to take nothin', old man. We're just borrowing your pasture for a bit."

"Like hell you are." Henry tried to turn and punch the much younger man. Santos easily knocked him down, and then, bending over, brought the butt of the shotgun down hard on the back of his skull with a crunch. Henry went limp on the ground.

Running up and seeing Henry Jessup on the ground, Tito recoiled at the sight. "What did you do?! He's just an old man. You said no one would be hurt. You said a quick in-and-out."

"Unforeseen circumstances," Santos shot back, smiling, a gold incisor shining in the moonlight. "Take the old man inside. I'll tend to him in a minute."

Richie and Tito grabbed the unconscious Henry under his arms and dragged him up the porch stairs and into his living room. They placed him, not too gently, into his old recliner, which sat in front of an ancient television.

Tito stood looking at Henry in his chair for a moment, "Sorry, old man. Shit, I hate this." Richie was pulling out drawers, looking for anything worth stealing. Tito slapped Richie on the arm, "Quit poking around. The old man ain't got two cents to put together." The men left the now-semiconscious and groaning man and went back outside.

Santos was leaning against the van and smoking a cigarette when the men came back. "Now we wait. You two stay here. I'll be right back," he said. He pulled himself away from the van and sauntered into the house. The silence was interrupted by a crash. Tito covered his ears when Henry screamed.

Santos was wiping his hands on a small kitchen towel as he walked back to the van. "What did you do, man?" Tito asked nervously.

"What I had to. I just convinced him to keep his mouth shut. You'd better shut up, too," Santos snarled. There was the distant sound of a plane engine. "Here they come."

The small plane skimmed the tops of the tall pines by the road—coming in slow and low. The plane didn't land, as Tito expected. Even in the semi-darkness, he could see a man push a large bundle out the small side door. The plane climbed back into the dark sky and headed off to the east.

The noise of a small plane engine disturbed the quiet night. Nora knew the sound of a Piper Malibu. It was the same small plane that her parents had flown. It was coming in low over the grove. She could hear the engine, which didn't seem quite right. It sounded like it was gliding, and then accelerating again. And one of the pistons was off a bit. A cold chill raced up her spine as her parent's crash crossed her mind.

She stood up, dislodging Hobo, her big silver tabby, who was curled up in her lap. Looking into the distance, she tried to spot the culprit that had interrupted her evening—spying its silhouette as it tipped its wings back and forth. Suddenly it dipped below the tree line, and she waited to hear the crash. The engine didn't stop, however, and there was no crash. She watched it reappear back in the night sky and fly away to the east.

Off in the distance, headlights from a car or a truck pierced the dark over on the Jessup's land. She followed the headlight beams as they moved, first to where she thought the plane would crash, and then back down the dirt track, to the main road. It was too dark and too far away to tell what kind of vehicle it was.

"How odd," she said, talking to the cat that was now winding around her legs. "Tomorrow morning,

I think I'll take Jasper and ride over to the Jessup's, and check if he's alright," she added—picking up her book and climbing the stairs. She was still uneasy once she got into bed, and had some trouble falling asleep.

The morning was shrouded in a light fog when Nora came down for breakfast.

"Ola," Rosita said, greeting her. "Once the fog burns off, the man on the television said it will be a nice clear day. That man that does the weather, he is very handsome. You need to find someone like that—a handsome man with a profession." She filled Nora's coffee cup and put a plate with a Spanish omelet and fresh biscuit in front of her

"You have been pushing me to get married since I was sixteen, Rosita," Nora laughed. "One of these days, I'll surprise you and do it. Or I could just become a nun, and then you won't have to worry about my love life at all."

"You know I love you like one of my own, chiquita. What about that nice sheriff who came to take Tito away? I saw the way you looked at each other. There is a fire there waiting to explode."

Nora almost choked on the piece of omelet in her mouth. "Waiting to explode? I'm not about to explode with anyone," she giggled.

Quickly changing the subject, she continued, "The doctor will be setting up some appointments for Gramps. If they call, just take whatever dates they give you. I want him checked over as soon as possible."

Rosita took a chair at the table with her coffee, "Did the doctor say if he thought something was wrong with him?"

"No, it's basically his age and working too hard. He needs to let me do more or hire someone for the office work. Maybe both. Rosita, did you hear that low-flying plane last night?" Nora asked—changing the subject.

"I heard it alright," Gramps interrupted, coming into the kitchen. "That darn fool almost scared me out of my bed and Rex, too. We were ready to duck into the closet or under the bed. Poor old Rex was shaking so bad I thought he'd shake his fur off."

"I was sitting out on the porch and listened to it coming in. It flew right down over the Jessup's pasture. I waited for the sound of a crash, but then it flew right back up and away again. It was strange. There were lights from a car or truck over there, too, and it left right after the plane did."

Gramps had his mouth full of Rosita's homemade biscuit, but still kept the conversation going. "It was probably some sky jockey showing off for his friends. Nothing for us to worry about," he mumbled around the breakfast he was still chewing.

"I'm going to take a ride over there and see if I find anything. I'd better check on Mr. Jessup while I'm there. He's all alone there at night."

"Good idea, girl," Gramps said. "Tell the old coot I said hi, and I'll be round once the oranges have been picked—another week or two maybe. I'll walk down to the packing house. You take the jeep."

Nora stood and took her empty plate to the sink. "No thanks, Gramps. I'm going to ride Jasper over. Pretty soon it will be too hot. He and I both need the exercise."

"Oh, exercise," Rosita said, throwing a dish cloth in the sink and turning to Nora. "You are too skinny now. A man wants something to hold onto. When I met Hector, he liked that I had a good figure. No man wants to make love to a pencil. They want a soft pillow to embrace. You put some meat on those bones, and you will get your man. I promise you."

Nora and Gramps tried to hold it in, but they both burst into gales of laughter. Glaring, Rosita stamped her foot, and took her ample frame out of the kitchen in a huff. But she stopped on the porch, and chuckled all to herself. She had helped raise Nora, and just as with her own children, she looked forward to grandchildren to spoil. She already had three grown children of her own and five grandchildren. Unfortunately, they were not living close and required a long plane ride to see them.

Jose was in Texas and worked for an oil company. Rita was in Chicago. Her husband worked for one of the big Chicago newspapers. She could never remember the name of it. Rosalinda was her youngest and a talented dancer. She was up in New York City, dancing her way around Broadway. She yearned for a baby to spoil. If only Nora would just cooperate, she thought. She walked off down to the little house she shared with Hector.

Chapter Six

Nora grabbed a full-brimmed felt hat off the peg by the door and walked out to the barn to saddle-up Jasper. "I'll see you at the packing house when I come back," she said.

"That leaves just you and me, old thing," Gramps said, scratching Rex behind the ears. The dog leaned into his knee with a look of contentment on his canine face.

"You fancy a ride to the packing house with me?" he asked Rex.

The dog ran from the old man to the door and then back again, wagging his tail. "An' they say dogs don't understand English, huh?"

Jasper heard Nora coming, and whinnied a welcome. She unlocked the tack room and grabbed his saddle and bridle. She mentally thanked her parents for having her ride English so many years ago. The saddle was a lot lighter than the traditional Western saddle common on the farms and ranches. Resting the saddle on a rack by the stall, she gave Jasper his breakfast and some clean water. While he ate, she cleaned out his stall, putting the old straw in a wheelbarrow for disposal later. Throwing clean new straw around the floor, she finished the job.

"Okay, Jasper," she said, slipping the bridle over his head. "Let's go for a ride and do some investigating."

Nora walked Jasper out to the mounting block, looking forward to her ride. The Jessups had been neighbors to the Hollisters forever. She felt bad that she hadn't visited more often. She would ride over and check up on Henry Jessup, make sure he was okay, and then see what she could find in the pasture near where she had seen the plane and the headlights.

Jasper was good as gold as she led him to the mounting block, climbed the steps and swung her leg over. Putting gentle pressure on his sides, she urged the horse forward. Soon, she was cantering along the back road that ran alongside both properties. She was surprised to find the gate to the Jessup place wide open. Not a good thing when there are cattle on the property. She got a foreboding feeling as she closed the gate behind her. Goose bumps and a chill made her shudder. Even Jasper was reluctant to move forward. Reaching the front of the farm house, she called out, "Henry, are you home? Henry Jessup. It's Nora Hollister." No answer.

She dismounted and tied Jasper to a branch of a nearby tree. "Henry, I'm coming in. Are you here?" Still there was no answer. Henry's shotgun lay at the bottom of the porch steps. She checked the chamber—still loaded. She picked up the gun, and pulled open the screen door, its old hinges squeaking.

The front room was dark. Heavy curtains covered the windows. Pulling them open one-by-one, she could see the room looked like a hurricane had been through it. It was then she noticed that Henry's recliner had blood on the arms and headrest. The cold chill came back, and she heard Jasper whinny. He was spooked, too. "Mr. Jessup, I'm here to help. It's Nora Hollister."

There was a trail of blood leading to the back of the house. Against her better judgment, she followed the drops to Henry's bedroom. The door was ajar. She slowly pushed it open, holding the shotgun ready in her hands. Her free hand flew to her mouth, stifling her scream. She almost dropped the gun. She wanted to run, but couldn't make herself move. Henry was on his bed . . . dead. He was on his back, blood obscuring the features of his face. It looked like someone had beaten the shit out of the old man. But why? He was just an old rancher who kept to himself, and never bothered a soul.

Nora backed out of the room and found her way to the phone in the hallway. Dialing 911, she tried to calm down enough to give the operator the details and get the sheriff. She was told not to leave and not to touch anything.

Sitting on the front porch steps with the shotgun across her lap, she put her head in her hands and cried tears of grief for her now-dead neighbor. The sheriff would be a while getting there, and she didn't want to be alone at this moment.

She went back into the house, and used the phone to call the packing house office. When Gramps answered, she told him what she had found.

"Oh my God! I'm sorry it had to be you that found him, Nora. I should have gone with you," Gramps said. "I'll come over straight away."

"Gramps, I think he was beaten to death. Who would do that to an old man?" she asked, wiping a tear from her eye.

"I don't know, Sweetheart, but we'll find out. I'm on my way." Gramps hung up the phone and walked out to Hector on the platform.

"I have to go over to the Jessup place for a bit. Take care of things here for me, will ya?" Gramps asked. Gramps went to his jeep and started the engine. Rex begged for a ride. "Not this time, Rex. I'll be back."

"Anything I can do?" Hector asked. It looked to him like something was wrong.

"Not right now, but thanks." Gramps took off and left—the dog watching him drive away down the road. Reaching the Jessup's back gate, he stopped the jeep and got out to open the gate. As he swung back the gate, his foot hit what he thought was a rock. Looking down, he saw a lock with a heavy chain attached. He picked it up, thinking old Jessup had lost it in the grass. Looking at it, he noticed that the hasp of the lock had been cut, maybe with a bolt cutter. Someone had come prepared and knew they would have to cut this lock off. Tossing the chain and lock in the back of the jeep, he pulled through and closed the gate behind him.

Nora watched as Gramps drove up, wheeled around the side of the house, and parked. She put down the gun and ran to her grandfather.

"Oh Gramps, it's awful," she cried. He gathered her into his arms and hugged her tight. Pushing away, she said, "I had time to think while I was waiting. What if this is connected to the plane and the car lights I saw last night?" She paced as she talked, walked over to Jasper, threw her arms around his neck and rested her forehead on his neck. Turning from her horse, "What if Henry confronted whoever it was? He had his gun out. I found it by the steps."

"That's for the sheriff to find out. Come sit down. They should be here soon."

Nora did as Gramps said. She picked the shotgun back up off the step and sat with it across her lap again. She didn't think anything was going to happen where she needed a shotgun; it just made her feel better to have it.

Chapter Seven

"Here they come," said Gramps, standing up to greet the sheriff. Nora looked up as Sheriff McAlister and a deputy got out of his car.

Oh great, here comes Sheriff Blue Eyes, she thought. Now try and keep your hormones in check, she chided herself. Even if you do want to do something naughty, someone has been murdered. This is a crime scene, for gosh sakes.

"We meet again, Nora," Gabe said. "I don't often get greeted by a pretty girl with a shotgun in her lap when I go out on a call."

Nora smiled slightly at the remark. She figured he was just trying to make her feel better. He moved slowly, and extended his hand to take the gun, which Nora gave up somewhat reluctantly.

"Are you okay?" he asked. Deep concern for her, and the situation she found herself in. showed in his eyes and on his face.

She stood and handed the gun to Gabe, stock first, barrel up. "It's loaded."

Gabe took the pump action gun and carefully unloaded it, ejecting all six shots on the ground. He turned to the deputy. "Alvarez, take the gun and pick up the shells. Have the crime lab look at it."

"I have something else for you to look at," Gramps took the lock and chain out of the back seat of the jeep. "I found these in the grass by the back gate. Someone used a bolt cutter on the lock."

More cars were pulling up, some with police officers, and some with medical personnel. Dr. Connors from the coroner's office came over to introduce himself. "Hello, Sheriff, I'm Doctor Connors. I haven't had a chance to meet you yet. I could have done without meeting you here, like this. Henry Jessup was an old friend of mine."

"Thanks for coming out," Gabe put his hand out and shook the man's hand.

"Stay here," Gabe said to Nora and Gramps. He took the crime scene officers inside along with the coroner.

Nora and her grandfather sat in silence, waiting. Gramps pulled out his old pocket watch to check the time. Finally, after what seemed like hours, but was really only a few minutes, Gabe returned, followed by a stretcher carrying the battered body of Henry Jessup. Nora turned her head into Gramps' shoulder to avoid looking at it.

"He was pretty beat up, but not enough to kill him," Dr. Connors said. "I'm guessing he had a heart attack or something. A younger man would have survived, but Jessup was in his eighties. I hope whoever did this is gonna roast in hell. I'll send you my report as soon as I can."

After talking to the coroner and issuing orders to the rest of the officers, Gabe returned to question Gramps and Nora. He stood with his hat in his hands, one foot resting on the bottom step.

"I'm very sorry about your friend. So, what made you come over here today?" He addressed his question to Nora.

"I came over to check up on Henry. Last night, I was sitting on the porch reading, before going up to bed. A plane flew over very low and caught my attention. After that, I saw some car lights in the pasture. It was late and didn't make any sense. I thought I better see if he was okay. It just seemed out of place to have lights in the pasture that late at night."

"You rode over here? Why not take the jeep?"

"Gramps was going to the packing house and needed the jeep. Besides, I like to ride Jasper when I can. I took the back road. I didn't expect to find this," she waved her hands in the direction of the house. "I thought maybe there was something wrong with his cattle. If his cattle were in trouble, maybe ours could be, too."

"Mr. Hollister, how did you come to be here?"

"Nora called me right after she called you guys. I came right over."

"How did you find the lock?"

"I came in the back way, too. I found it when I got out of the car to open the gate."

"The gate was open when I first came over. Ranchers and farmers don't leave gates open. I closed it behind me. It's a common courtesy around here," Nora offered.

"I see. I'm new around here, as you know. I'm a big city boy, transferred here from Tampa. I need all the help I can get to understand how things work here," Gabe commented. "Well, I guess that's all I need for now. Can I come around with more questions if I have any?" He was looking straight at Nora. She wanted to go swimming in those eyes.

"Sure, come around any time. Can I call you . . . if I see anything suspicious—that is?" she stammered.

"Sure, by all means." He walked her over to Jasper. "Can I give you a hand up?"

"Does the city boy know how?"

"No, so just tell me what I need to do," he said, with an adorably goofy smile on his face.

She had to laugh, and his smile set her heart fluttering.

Nora turned, facing Jasper's side. Grabbing the pommel and the cantle of the saddle, she raised her left leg. "Just lift," she instructed Gabe.

He did as he was told. As she rose, she threw her right leg over, and settled softly in the saddle. Picking up the reins, she said, "I'll teach you to ride, if you want. It might come in handy around here. Lots of places you can't get to by car."

He placed his hand on her thigh. She felt the heat through her jeans. A little inappropriate, she thought, but who cares. She certainly didn't.

"I'd love a ride with you. I mean yes, I'd love to learn to ride," Gabe said, getting lost by her chestnut hair catching the sun and her hazel eyes flashing topaz sparks as she looked down at him from her saddle.

As she turned Jasper towards home, she was pleased to note that Sheriff Blue Eyes was blushing.

Gramps had been keeping an eagle eye on what was going on. He walked up beside Gabe. "Should I be asking about your intentions toward my granddaughter? Directing his question to Gabe, he raised his eyebrows. "I'm old, but I'm not blind."

"Mr. Hollister, I'll be honest. As soon as I figure out my intentions, you will be the first to know."

"Fair enough," Gramps said, seating his large frame in the jeep. Gabe stood, watching as the older man drove back out the way he had come.

Gabe settled his hat squarely on his head and went back in the house. He had a crime to solve, and looking over the scene again on his own might give him some answers—or not.

He walked up to the steps and tried to recreate what might have happened in his mind. The gun was found fully loaded out here. Henry Jessup was found in his bedroom. There was blood on his chair in the living room. It all added up to the fact that Henry had taken his gun with him when he went to check on something.

Someone must have surprised him because he never got off a shot. Or he knew the person who had approached him. More questions than answers came to Gabe as he looked at the blood on the chair and the old man's bed. His mind was spinning as he started walking down to the pasture where Nora said she had seen the lights.

He was trying to stay in the shade of the tree line. He was half way down when he saw the tracks of a vehicle in the sparse grass. Nora had been right. There was a car here last night. He walked out into the open. There was a depression where something heavy had landed hard. *What the hell was going on out here?*

He took off his Stetson and wiped his forehead with an old handkerchief from his pocket. Placing his hat back on his head, he walked back to the house and his car.

Chapter Eight

A week later the coroner called Sheriff McAlister with his report. "What's up, Doc?" Gabe said and laughed. "I always wanted to say that."

"Yeah, yeah, like I haven't heard that one before," Dr. Connors answered. He sounded aggravated, so Gabe got down to business.

"I got more of the lab results in today. Henry Jessup was murdered, although probably not intentionally. Like I said at the beginning, a younger, fitter man would most likely have survived. Henry suffered a broken nose, black eye and the kicker was a posterior fossa hematoma, where the blood pools in the intracranial cavity," the doctor concluded.

"Okay the first bit I got, but explain that posterior thing."

"I believe he got hit on the head—which knocked him out. Whoever it was got him inside, and when Henry came to, someone slapped him around, but the damage was already done. He was bleeding into his brain. He would have been able to walk to his room, thinking he only needed to rest, but he was already dying."

"Jesu, Doc, the poor guy."

"He just went to sleep and never woke up. Unfortunately, it's not that uncommon. Even if he did survive the night, he was walking around with a time bomb in his head. I talked to Dr. Winters. Henry was on Coumadin for a slight heart problem."

Sitting on the edge of his desk, Gabe asked. "What's that Coumadin stuff do?"

"It's an anti-coagulant. His blood would be slow to clot. He bled-out in his brain, and that's also why his broken nose and that cut near his eye bled so badly."

"Thanks for filling me in. Let me know if anything else pops up."

"Sure thing, Sheriff."

After the doctor hung up, Gabe sat back down at his desk. His head was down, elbows on the desk, resting his chin on his clenched hands, deep in thought. At the sound of a polite knock on his open door, he looked up and was surprised to see Nora standing there.

"What brings you to town, Nora? Must say I'm glad, though, whatever it is."

"I think I left out something important the other day.

"Have a seat," he said, pulling a scarred-up office chair over to his desk. "Can I get you a coffee, a cold drink, water?" he asked.

"No, thanks, I'm good," she answered—*manners and good looking, hmmm.* "Gramps is picking up a couple of things so I have to be quick. I forgot to tell you there was a plane that night."

"A plane?" he asked.

"I was sitting on the porch reading. The plane was coming in low, too low. I thought it was going to crash. It flew right over Jessup's and back up. It didn't have time to land. That's how I saw the lights. I was looking for the plane."

"Any chance you saw any lettering or numbers?"

"No. It was too dark, but I do know it was a Piper Malibu."

"How do you know it was a Piper Malibu?" he asked.

"My dad had one. I know the sound of the engine. He and my mom actually died when it crashed a couple of years ago."

"I'm sorry, Nora," he said and meant it.

"I haven't flown since that day."

"I'm guessing you have a pilot's license?"

"Yes. I had just passed my solo for the license. I would have been with them, but Jasper was getting new shoes that day.

Gabe was becoming more and more intrigued by the minute. Not only beautiful but . . . she had a head on her shoulders and used it. The combination fascinated him.

"Look, I've got to go meet Gramps. I hope the information helps."

"Yes, it does. Thanks for dropping by. I'm going to make a couple of calls and get back to you," Gabe said and thought quickly. "Can I come out later tonight, and you can show me the route the plane took as it came and went? Maybe sit on that porch of yours for a while. In case it comes back."

"I think that might be okay. You have to get the facts right, don't you?" Nora said.

"You said you were on your porch? About what time was that?"

"It must have been around nine or so."

"Right," he said. He was looking in her eyes and not down at his note book.

"Gramps is waiting, so bye for now." She turned and hurried away before she changed her mind.

Gabe stood there and watched her go. "Crap," he muttered out loud, watching the sway of her hips. He rubbed his hands over his face. An idea was turning around in his head . . . actually two ideas: one about the plane and the other about Nora. He went back to sit at his desk and shuffled through an old notebook he kept with phone numbers he had hoped he would never have to use down here in the land of cows and oranges.

Chapter Nine

Gramps answered the knock on the door, "Hi, Sheriff, come on in. Nora is already out on the porch. Are you off duty?"

Gabe stepped in and took off his hat, nervously turning it in his hands. "I'm off, but you never know."

"Can I get you a beer or maybe just a soft drink?" Gramps asked.

"I'll take the beer, thanks Mr. Hollister," Gabe said to the old man's back as he dug in the fridge for the beer.

"Oh, for pity sake, just call me 'Gramps.' Everyone else around here does."

"Only if you call me Gabe," he said taking the offered beer in his hand. He stood there awkwardly, the beer in one hand, his hat in the other.

"That's a deal. Come on, I'll take you out to the porch and Nora."

The two men found Nora peacefully reading in the soft glow of a lamp. Gabe appreciated the way the light made her hair glow with streaks of russet and gold. When the wooden planks of the porch creaked, she turned. "You made it," she said putting her book down. "Have a seat. It might be a waste of time waiting for that plane to come again."

Gramps retreated to the kitchen. Gabe moved a rather large cat out of a chair next to Nora. "Sorry, Cat," he said. The cat sat on the floor in front of Gabe looking at him as if to say, "Who do you think you are taking my seat?" Hobo then stood, stretched and walked away with is tail in the air.

"Hobo doesn't mind. He's always getting in the way."

"Nice cat, though," Gabe replied. Sitting down, he placed his hat on the floor next to his chair, opened his beer, and took a long pull on the cold brew. "That's good after the day I've had."

"Bad day, huh?" Nora asked.

"It started off really good when you came by for a visit. It went downhill after that." Gabe sipped his beer wondering how much he should tell her about what he'd found out. Deciding to tell her everything, he started at the beginning.

"After you left, I thought about that plane some more. I'd read an article somewhere, probably in a police journal, that said the drug cartels were moving north from Miami. It said that the dealers are dropping their loads in Lake Okeechobee. Pick-up men take speed boats out and pick them up before they sink.

"There is a group they are calling the 'Okeechobee Eight' that the Feds are trying to catch and prosecute. There might be a whole bunch involved, but that's the main group.

"It made me think about the plane you saw and the headlights. It would also explain why Henry Jessup was attacked. If it's what I think, they couldn't afford a confrontation with an old man who might go to the police. They roughed him up, threatened him to keep his mouth shut. They didn't expect him to die on them. Of course, I'm just taking some educated guesses right now."

"Who are they?" Nora asked.

"For the answer to that I had to call a friend of mine in the DEA, the Drug Enforcement Agency, up in Washington, D.C. He didn't want to talk on the phone, so he's coming down in the next couple of days. He thinks there might be something big starting up around here."

"Big? You mean like a big drug thing going on around here? Gabe, this is Myakka. Nothing big goes on around here, ever. We're in the middle of nowhere."

"Maybe not, but he wants to come down anyway. It's all . . ."

"Shush, listen." Nora cut him off. "Don't you hear it?"

Gabe strained to hear what she heard. Then from the south came the sound of a plane engine. Nora reached out her hand and grabbed Gabe's arm. Listening carefully, she said, "That's the same plane from the other night."

"How can you tell?" he asked softly.

"One of the pistons is misfiring."

Gabe would just have to trust her on that one. Nora turned off her reading lamp, and they both stood, watching and waiting. The plane came closer, and just as it had the other night, it swooped down low over Jessup's pasture and rose right up again. Headlights came on as the plane rose. The lights seemed to move towards where the plane had dropped. The sound of car doors slamming echoed in the still air. Suddenly another sound split the quiet evening.

"You shot Richie! What in hell did you do that for?" Tito exclaimed.

"You're next if you don't move this shit and load it in the van," Santos said, pointing a gun at Tito's head.

"Okay! Okay! But why shoot him?" Tito asked.

"He was helping himself a bit too often. I don't take that from anyone. Remember that, in case you every think about cheating me. Besides, you think he was in jail with you because he was an angel?

"We've been bringing this stuff in for a couple of months now. Richie was too sure of himself and got caught dealing. That's how he ended up with you. We took him out so he couldn't talk to anyone about us. Now, he definitely won't talk." Santos laughed at his own joke.

"Now, move your boney ass. Someone might have heard that shot and come calling."

Tito threw heavy packages of cocaine in the back of the van as fast as he could. The two men jumped in and sped out the open back gates.

"That was a gun shot," Gabe exclaimed. He looked around for his hat. Hobo had found a new place to sleep, curled up in it. He dumped the cat out, slapping the hat against his leg to get rid of the fur.

He raced out the way he had come, passing a very confused and curious Gramps. Nora was hot on his tail. He was jumping into the driver's side of his car when Nora pulled open the passenger side and started to get in as well. "You have to stay here. It might not be safe."

"Oh, I'll be safe alright," Nora said. It was then she showed him the rifle in her hands. "All loaded and ready to go."

Gabe didn't wait to argue and started the engine. Nora never ceased to amaze him. The idea crossed his mind he might have to have that talk with Gramps sooner than he thought.

They drove out the back way. Jessup's gate had been left open again. Driving away, the red tail lights of a vehicle disappeared down the road.

Continuing through the gate, they stopped the car by the old house, got out and shut the doors quietly in case anyone was still around. Gabe turned on a flashlight, keeping it pointed at the ground as they made their way down the tree line.

"There's no vehicle here. That must have been them leaving," Nora said. She kept walking around in the pasture.

"You're probably right. We'll have to come back in the daylight to find anything."

"Oh, hell," Nora stumbled and fell, the rifle flying from her hand.

"Are you okay?" Gabe asked, trying to find her with the flashlight in the dark.

"I think I landed in a cow patty," she said standing up. She was making a face and shaking her hands in disgust.

"I don't think it was a cow patty, Nora," Gabe said, shining his flashlight on a body and then on Nora's hands, which were covered in blood.

"Ooooh . . . ," Nora squealed looking at her hands. She bent over and tried to wipe the blood from her hands in the grass.

Gabe was leaning over the dead man. He turned him over and recognized him immediately. The dead man was Richie Cantura. "That's the guy that helped Tito post bail. What the hell is going on here?" he asked, taking Nora by the elbow, and walking her back to his car.

He called into headquarters to report what they had found and get some help on the way. He dug around in his trunk and handed Nora a semi-clean rag to wipe her hands with.

"Can I go in the house and give Gramps a call?" she asked. "He'll want to know that we're okay and that we might be a while." She looked at her hands, "And I need to wash my hands."

"This is still a crime scene, so don't touch anything else," Gabe cautioned.

By the time she returned, flashing lights from several patrol cars were coming up the dirt tract from the main road.

"The first officer to arrive will take you and your rifle home," Gabe said.

"Thanks," she said. "I really want to take a shower." She was holding her hands away from her clothes. Her quick hand wash had still left clotted blood under her nails, and looking at them made her shudder.

It didn't take long for Officer Alvarez to arrive. He took notice of Nora standing beside Sheriff McAlister. "Ma'am," he said touching the brim of his Stetson in greeting.

"Would you please give Miss Hollister a ride home?" Gabe asked. "Come right back, and we'll go over the crime scene as best we can in the dark. Is the coroner on his way?"

"Yes, Sir, I called him right after I spoke with you." He turned to Nora, "This way, Ma'am," he said gesturing towards his patrol car.

Nora looked back at Gabe as she walked behind Officer Alvarez. Making a face, she mouthed the words —"I'm a Ma'am? Ma'am?" She pointed at herself. Gabe had to try very hard to suppress a laugh. He knew in that moment that he was a goner.

In no time, she was back in her own house and pounding up the stairs to take a shower. Gramps tried to talk to her as she flew past him.

"I'll be down in a jiffy and fill you in. Right now, I need a shower, badly."

A few minutes later, she came down wrapped in a comfy robe, her hair still wet as she rubbed it with a towel.

Gramps was in the kitchen waiting for her to tell him what had happened.

"Gramps, I need a drink," she said.

"It was that bad, huh? You're in luck. I have a bottle of Macallan tucked away." While Gramps went to retrieve the Scotch, Nora talked to Rex and rubbed his ears.

"What is going on around here, Rex, Old Boy? Two dead bodies, and Gabe thinks there are drug dealers around here now."

Gramps came back with two glasses filled with about an inch of the honey-gold whiskey. Nora took her glass and raised it in salute, "Thanks, Gramps." The potent liquor burned all the way down and warmed her insides. She closed her eyes a moment to collect her thoughts. She told her grandfather about how they had found Richie Cantura.

"If it is drug dealers, I bet that Richie person got greedy and whoever it is running this put a permanent stop to it," Gramps said, draining his glass.

Nora took another sip. "I'm going to bed. I just can't get my head around all this. First, Henry Jessup, and now another man is dead. Gabe will be by in the morning. I have to make a statement, again." She finished her drink and took both glasses to the sink. Talking out loud to herself she said, "I've just got to stop finding dead bodies," and walked up the stairs to bed.

Her sleep was disturbed by dreams and nightmares that had her tossing and turning. She woke with a start. She had been falling into a blood-filled pool where Richie's face looked at her.

What disturbed her more were the other dreams she'd had. Sensual dreams of her in Gabe's embrace. She looked to him for comfort and to make sense of everything, yet her body responded to his arms holding her—his lips seeking hers.

She woke up again. Still the feelings insisted on staying with her. She felt her dampened desires were taking over and she had no control. She'd had brief affairs in college, but she was never, ever lost in this consuming desire to have her dreams come true. What would Gabe think if he knew? They barely knew each other.

Waiting for the crime scene crew to finish, Gabe had stayed at the scene long after midnight. He drove to his small house in Arcadia, tired and worn out. He tried to sleep, but it eluded him. His mind kept going over and over the events of the last few days. He hoped his friend in the DEA was on his way. He'd call and check in the morning. Once that decision was made, he tried for sleep again.

Not much luck there. This time, his thoughts turned to Nora and the way the light made her eyes change color. They could be gray and smoldering or tawny as a lion. Her smile was magical, and he longed to kiss her lips and explore her mouth with his. His body took his thoughts and was responding. As the sun started its ascent, he gave up on getting any rest and took a cold shower.

Chapter Ten

Gabe hung up the phone after talking with his friend, Daniel Parker. He was on his way and would arrive in a couple of hours. Gabe had some time before he needed to set out for the Tampa Airport. He didn't know why, but he found himself at Nora's back door first.

"Hi, Gabe. I thought you might stop by this morning," Gramps said pushing the screen door open. "Come on in. How about a cup of coffee?"

"Thanks, Gramps, but I don't really have time. I came by to see if Nora cared to take a ride with me to the airport. I'm picking up that friend from the DEA I told you all about."

"Why not go ask her?" Gramps suggested. "She's out in the barn feeding Jasper." He smiled as

Gabe bounced down the steps and quickly walked out to the barn.

He found Nora, pitchfork in hand, cleaning out Jasper's stall while the big Appaloosa, tied to a ring on the wall outside in the walkway, finished his breakfast. Jasper whinnied as Gabe entered the barn. Nora came out of the stall and brushed damp hair off her face. She smiled at Gabe and stood there leaning on the pitchfork, hay in her hair and muck on her boots. He thought she was the most beautiful creature he had ever seen.

Walking around Jasper, he prudently took the pitchfork from her hands."I never kiss anyone while they are holding a deadly weapon," Gabe said taking her in his arms.

Nora never had time to think of protesting. His kiss was soft and sweet. He was drawing back when she snaked her arms around and brought him back. Her lips were on fire as they took his. Needing to take a breath, they stepped back from each other, happy—although a bit confused. What had they begun? Was this even a beginning? Their thoughts echoed each other.

"Aaaa, I don't know why I did that," Gabe said. "I just couldn't resist."

"I'm glad you did," Nora answered shyly. She felt the heat rising in her face.

"Can you take a ride with me? I'm picking up my friend Daniel Parker at the airport in Tampa. He's with the DEA. We can fill him in on the way back."

"I have to put Jasper away, and I smell," Nora said, trying to brush the straw from her hair.

"I'll leave the windows open, and you look fine to me."

"Give me two minutes, and I'll be ready." Nora said, quickly untying Jasper and leading him into his stall. "Can you take the hose and fill his water pail? I'll meet you at your car."

She rushed off leaving Gabe wondering where the hose was and how to fill the water pail. By the time he figured it out and walked out to his car, she was waiting. She'd changed out of her smelly boots and combed the straw out of her hair. In minutes they were off, traveling north to Tampa and the airport.

Showing his badge to a security guard, Gabe parked his patrol car outside the arrivals' terminal. Reading the gate announcements posted over the baggage carousels, they made their way to the one offloading from Washington, D.C. Daniel was already there waiting for his things to show up.

Gabe stole up behind him and surprised Daniel, grabbing his arm and spinning him around into a friendly guy hug. "How're you doing old man," Gabe joked.

Daniel was in his early thirties, although his hair showed traces of early gray. He was easy to look at and very fit—although not quite as tall as Gabe. He had his suit jacket over his arm and was carrying an overstuffed briefcase.

Daniel found his bag coming around and hefted it off the carousel before it could go around again. He placed in on the floor in front of him. "Who's the pretty lady?"

"Dan, this is my friend, Nora Hollister," Gabe introduced them.

"I'm pleased to meet you, Ma'am."

"Nice to have you come and give us a hand down here," Nora said. "But it's Nora. I swear I'll shoot the next person that calls me Ma'am."

"Beauty and a sense of humor, too," Dan laughed.

"Don't be fooled. She means it. She carries a rifle at home."

"Only sometimes," Nora smiled. "And don't forget the pitchfork."

Nora and Gabe exchanged a knowing look. Dan raised his eyebrows, "Mmm. Anything I should know about?"

"No." they said at the same time, laughing at the memory.

Heading back to Myakka and the grove, Gabe and Nora filled Dan in with more details on what was happening.

"I looked into the Cartels and found that you just might be right. Pablo Escobar runs the Medellin Cartel out of Columbia. Escobar has been trying to move his operations further north. It's getting too hot in Okeechobee. We're looking into rounding up his players there. Escobar stays in Columbia, so we can't get to him. He pays a lot of money to fight extradition. I'd sure like to put pressure on him by putting some of his operations out of business, though."

"How can he get away with this? Surely his own country can put him out of business," Nora said stunned that such a criminal could exist.

"Escobar is clever and ruthless. Whoever opposes him is killed. It doesn't matter who. Police and politicians are gunned down in the street. He had the police station itself blown up. He gives money to social programs for the poor and soccer clubs for the kids. He wants to be a leader of the country. One of his political opponents was assassinated recently. He's worth a ton of money. They say he bought a Lear jet just to move his money around. All from cocaine smuggled into the States," Daniel said. "It's estimated that 15 tons of cocaine are smuggled in each day."

"That's crazy," Nora said. She could not believe that one man controlled so much.

"I'd be happy if we can just catch the men that killed Henry Jessup and Richie Cantura," Gabe said. Traffic was light, and they made good time. They arrived back at Nora's in the late afternoon. The sun was setting, and the slight breeze had dust devils swirling in the sandy yard.

Rex came off the porch where he had been dozing in the sun. Gramps heard him barking and stepped out. "Quiet, Rex," he yelled at the old dog. "Who have you got here?" he asked— extending his hand to Daniel.

Nora made the introductions to Rosita and Gramps. The older man asked them inside. "Nice to have you come down and give us a hand, Daniel. Come on in and have a cold drink."

Rosita was busy at the stove stirring and adding spices to her cooking pots.

"Thanks, I'm happy to help. I'd like to take a look at the crime scene and get a feel for what's going on. Like I told Gabe and Nora, I believe that cocaine is being dropped from that plane. The cars are picking it up and taking it to be distributed. Mr.

Jessup might have confronted them, and they beat him to shut him up. I'm not sure about your man Richie. He might have been skimming and got caught. You say he was just bailed out with another guy?"

"Yeah, a guy named Tito. He was locked up for fraud. He was falsifying the grove's records. You know, I'm surprised they tried again after Mr. Jessup was found dead. They must have known the police would be called in," Gabe said. He took a glass of iced tea from Gramps and handed one to Dan.

"They don't care. They'll shoot and kill anyone that gets in their way." Dan took a drink from the cold tea. "Thanks, this hits the spot."

Gramps put the jug back in the fridge and told Dan, "I'm wrapping up the season this week. I'll pay the workers off and give out a couple of bonuses, and they can move on. They're good people trying to make a living. I don't want anyone else hurt," Gramps said.

"That might be a good idea," Daniel agreed.

"I'll tell Hector, my foreman, to let them know tomorrow and have payroll get the money ready for Friday. There's only about a week left anyway. They can move on over the weekend." Gramps had it all figured out.

"That's good," Gabe agreed. "And thanks for the tea. I guess I'll see you all later then. I'll take Dan over to Jessup's before the sun sets." Gabe put his hat back on his head and looked at Nora. He wanted to sit with her again on the porch and not have to talk about drugs and dead bodies. He was thinking he could sit beside her forever, and that scared him more than the drug cartel did.

Nora stood on the back steps and followed Gabe's car until the tail lights turned onto the main road. Rosita called her back in to set the table for supper. Rosita was humming a little tune as she stirred rice on the stove.

"Don't you go thinking what you're thinking. I've only just met him," Nora said.

Rosita smiled. "Who says I'm thinking anything?" she asked, placing the rice and Carne Asada on the table. She knew this was one of Nora's favorites. She was a talented cook, taking recipes from Mexico, Cuba, Porto Rico and her home country of Columbia. She made them her own way, often adding the citrus flavors of Florida.

The light was fading fast as Gabe and Dan walked back to the patrol car. They had searched the field as best as they could. Jessup's cattle had been moved to another pasture until his son Ralph could figure out what to do with them. Ralph was not a farmer. He lived in Sarasota and worked in a bank. Gabe figured the place would be put up for sale and bought by some city guy who wanted to play farmer. It was happening all over these days.

"This is just the kind of place the cartel would use for its drop. An old man they figured they could control. A quick in-and-out and no one the wiser," Dan said, sliding into the passenger seat.

"I'm worried about Nora and her grandfather," Gabe said, putting the car in gear and turning around.

"They should be fine as long as they don't get in the way or interfere."

"Somehow, I don't think Nora is going to follow that advice," Gabe said. He was thinking about how Nora had followed him, rifle and all. She would not back down easily. As much as he admired her courage, he was afraid it could get her into a lot of trouble.

Gabe took Dan back to his small house in Arcadia. It was a Craftsman style with three bedrooms upstairs. Dan was shown to the one Gabe kept for guests, not that he had many. His folks still lived up in Tampa, and they could visit without having to stay over. Usually Gabe went up to them. When he did, his sister and her family would come over. Gabe's dad used any excuse to barbeque something. His mom loved the family gatherings. Her one thing was family. Her children and grandchildren were her pride and joy.

Gabe didn't think he would be able to get away for a while, with all that was going on now. He thought he would like to take Nora with him the next time he went to visit. His mom was going to love her, and his dad would admire her spunk.

After showing Dan where to find some towels for a shower, he went down to fix supper. Looking in the fridge, he didn't see many options. A box of dried pasta and a jar of sauce was Gabe's go-to for a quick meal.

Dan came down the stairs, toweling his hair, still wet from his shower. He looked a lot more comfortable in his worn gym pants and t-shirt, than he did in his suit and tie.

"How do you guys survive down here in this heat?" he asked, taking the edge of the towel off his neck to wipe the sweat dripping down his forehead.

"You think this is bad? This is the best time of year down here," Gabe said. He turned on an air conditioner in a side window. "That should help in a bit."

Dan lifted the lids of the pots on the stove. "You have to get a cookbook, Gabe. That's the same stuff you cooked in college. Remember the time you forgot to turn off the stuff you were cooking in the dorm room? The smoke was billowing down the hall, alarms going off. You came back from the library just as the fire department arrived. You almost got thrown out of the dorms for that one." Dan sat back in a kitchen chair, smiling. "Remember the no cooking rule which you ignored all the time?

"When we were in college, I thought we would both go for the FBI. I did and ended up in the DEA. How come you went for the Sheriff's Department?" Dan asked. He'd stretched-out his tall frame and leaned back in the chair.

Gabe went to the fridge and took out a couple of cold beers, placing one in front of Dan, opening the other for himself.

"Remember in our last year, my mom got sick? You were the only one I told about her breast cancer," Gabe started to explain. "I wanted to stay close to home, you know, just in case. The Sheriff's Office was a way to stay close to Tampa and still be in law enforcement. She got better, and I found that I enjoyed doing what I was doing."

"Okay, I get it. But why transfer down here to Crackerville?" Dan joked.

"Crackerville? Really." Gabe raised his brows at the remark. "There are a couple of reasons. I get to be more than I could be up there. Here, I'm in charge of the department. It's small, and I get to know my deputies, their families and what they're capable of. I like knowing people's names down here. I'm dealing with real people, not just names on a report. And another thing, I like Crackerville. They have a long, strong heritage.

"The name Cracker goes back to the times when they drove the cattle and horses from one coast to the other—right through this area here. They called it the 'Cracker Trail.' The cowboys were called crackers because of the sound their whips made. It's living history here. Families have been here for generations. I hope to have roots that deep someday."

Dan got curious and asked, "So what's the deal with you and Nora? Have you staked a claim yet?"

"I'm working on it," Gabe admitted, remembering the kiss in the barn.

"Better work a bit faster before someone beats you to it."

"By someone . . . do you mean you?"

"Only if she's up for grabs, pal."

"Guess I'd better work a little faster then."

Dan had a thoughtful look on his face. "Maybe you'll plant that tree with deep roots with Miss Hollister."

"Maybe," Gabe answered. "Enough of all that, let's eat." He stood and took his plate to the stove, effectively ending that particular conversation.

The men helped themselves, filling their plates from the pots on the stove. They talked about their old college days and who remembered who. Then the conversation got serious and turned to what was happening with the drugs and the cartel moving in.

"I have to do whatever I can to stop drugs coming in through my area. They must have someone local—someone who knows the area. How did they pick Jessup's place for a drop? How often are they making the drop?"

Dan stifled a yawn. "Those are great questions for the morning. I'm beat." Being a good guest, he took his plate to the sink and washed it along with Gabe's. The pots were set to soak, and the two men found their way to bed.

Gabe lay awake for a while listening to an owl hooting in a gnarled oak behind his house. His thoughts were like turning pages in a book— quickly jumping from the drug cartel to Nora and back again.

Chapter Eleven

Tito knew his way around the grove in the dark. He parked his late model truck down by the tractor shed and stayed in the shadows as he made his way to the packing plant. The truck was hidden from anyone up at the house.

He still had a couple of friends who worked the Hollister grove, and he'd found out about tomorrow being the last day for the workers. He needed money fast. After what had happened to Richie, he wanted to run as far away as possible from what was going down around here.

He knew there would be pay packets left out on the old man's desk. He figured there might be a couple of thousand there, counting the bonuses and everything being paid out.

Stealing through the darkness, he came to the back of the plant. Stacking some wooden orange crates up to a back window, he climbed up and peered in. A light glowed from the office. "Old man can't even remember to turn out the lights," he muttered to himself.

Easing the window open, trying not to let it squeak, he squeezed his body in. As soon as his feet hit the floor, the old boards creaked. He stood still as a statue expecting someone to challenge him. His nerves had him sweating. He rubbed the sting of it out of his eyes with his shirt.

One foot in front of the other, cringing as the old boards creaked, he crept across the packing house floor towards the office. He was supposed to be alone, but somehow, he knew he wasn't. The hair on the back of his neck was tingling.

Rex came out of the office. His nails clattering on the wooden floor, tail wagging, he went to greet the visitor. Tito was not a favorite of the old dog, but Rex took any scratch behind the ears he could get.

"Yeah, yeah," Tito whispered giving the dog a mindless scratch behind his ears while keeping his eyes on the office door. The dog flopped onto his back hoping for a belly rub. He was disappointed when Tito moved away and stood beside the office door, out of sight.

"Rex," Gramps called to the dog. "I guess you're telling me it's time to go home. I'm so stiff from sitting I can hardly move." Gramps stood, moving his shoulders to get the stiffness out. "Come on, old thing, we can finish up in the morning. I'll have to show Nora how to do this paperwork I guess."

Gramps walked out of the office and looked at Rex sitting in the middle of the room. The dog had his head cocked to the side as if trying to figure something out. "What's got into you?" he asked—right before he caught movement out of the corner of his eye and the world went black.

"Why did you have to be here tonight, old man?" Tito asked the unconscious man on the floor. The dog looked up at Tito and back to Gramps on the floor. He seemed to be asking "What did you do that for?"

"Sorry dog, but I got big trouble on my ass." He stepped over the man on the floor and made a beeline for the packets on the desk. He stuffed them quickly in his jeans and inside his shirt as fast as he could. Ruffling through the desk drawers in case there was anything of value, he noticed Gramps had left his pocket watch by the lamp. "I need this more than you do right now. It might be worth a few bucks."

Making his escape through the side door, he drove with his headlights off until he reached the main road. Any other state but Florida was looking pretty good right now. He had to get away from that psycho Santos and whatever he was mixed up in. Tito wanted no part of it, no matter how good the money was. The man scared the shit out of him.

Nora looked up from her book. Her grandfather was taking a long time down at the packing house. It was a nice evening, so she decided to walk down to the plant and surprise him. Dislodging Hobo from her lap, she went to the kitchen and filling a thermos with iced tea, took her hat off the peg and headed out.

It was a bright night with the full moon shining high in the sky. She loved seeing so many stars and tried to pick out a constellation or two while walking. You didn't see so many stars in towns and cities. The cicadas were buzzing in the trees. Bats from a roost in the old barn were out hunting for their supper.

Even before she saw the side door standing wide open, she knew something was wrong. Seeing the door open was strange because Gramps hated letting the mosquitoes in. Climbing the steps, she called out, "Gramps, it's Nora. You know you left the door open. Don't come complaining to me about mosquito bites. Rex came wagging his tail, his tongue hanging out. "Need some water in your bowl, boy?" she asked the old dog. She walked across the plant floor, head down rubbing the dog's soft ears.

"Gramps, Rex needs some water. What have you been doing in here?" Looking up, she stopped, seeing her grandfather slumped on the floor outside his office. She ran over and heard the old man moan. Helping him sit up, she saw the bloody gash on the side of his head.

"What happened? Did you fall? I'm calling Doc Winters." Nora stood and went to the phone on the desk.

"Someone hit me." She heard Gramps say weakly.

"What?" She couldn't believe what she heard.

She knelt beside him. "Who hit you?"

"Didn't see him."

Nora phoned Gabe, getting him out of bed and then Doc Winters. Gabe said he would be there right away. Doc was out on another call, but his service would reach him.

Rex was getting in the way when she tried to get her grandfather up and to his chair behind the desk. The more she pushed the dog away the more he wanted to help. Tears of frustration, anger and fear ran down her face. Finally, she managed. It was then she noticed that the tray they kept the pay packets in was empty.

She filled a glass with cold tea from the thermos and helped her grandfather drink a bit, "Thanks girl, that's a bit better."

Leaving her grandfather, she went out to the first aid box and took out a few packets of gauze pads. She quickly brought them back, opened a couple and made a compress for the old man's head wound. "Hold this," she ordered.

After filling the dog's water bowl from the water cooler in the corner she asked, "Gramps, did you get the wages for the field workers today?"

"Yeah, Helen brought them over late this afternoon. I was just finishing up adding a bit for the bonuses."

"Gramps, the tray is empty. Someone took all the packets. That person is the one who hit you."

"Aw, shit," Gramps muttered.

Nora took the compress from his head and changed it for a clean one. Gramps was done with her fussing and waved her hand away. "I'm fine," he said taking the pad from her and holding it to his head himself.

"You're not fine. You've just been hit on the head." She felt her eyes filling with tears.

"It's a hard head," he countered.

A siren coming to a halt outside had Rex bounding for the door. The sound of heavy boots coming up the stairs reached the office, and Nora relaxed knowing help had arrived.

"Can't stay out of trouble, can you?" Gabe asked standing in the doorway, one hand on his gun and the other leaning on the door frame. He was just about the best-looking thing Nora had ever seen. She stood and ran to him—tears running down her face. He gathered her into his arms and planted a gentle kiss on her head.

"It's not her this time," Gramps laughed. He took the cloth off his head and showed Gabe his wound.

"Ow, that's got to hurt," Gabe said. "How much do you remember about what happened tonight?"

"I called Doc Winters, and he'll get here when he can," Nora said to Gabe.

"I told you I don't need that quack," Gramps grumbled.

"He's coming, and that's that," she replied sternly. "If you don't behave, I'll call Nurse Hill, too."

"Not that old battle ax, please," Gramps huffed and found something in his iced tea more interesting than arguing with Nora.

"Gramps, tell me what happened," Gabe coaxed.

"I was putting the bonus in the packets for the workers tomorrow. I had a couple of other things to take care of, too. This place don't run itself. You'll figure that out quick enough." He aimed that part at Nora.

"Rex heard something and took a walk out the door. I didn't hear him bark like he would if it was a stranger, so I thought he spied a mouse or maybe a rat or raccoon. They do come around at night. Well, I decided to stretch a bit before I quit for the night and followed Rex out and called to him. He was just sitting there with this pleased look on his face.

I took another step, and that's when I got hit. I got blindsided and didn't see who hit me, but Rex knew him. I'm sure of it."

More footfalls sounded, and Doc Winters appeared in the doorway.

"What some people won't do for a house call," Doc said, walking into the office. He placed his black bag on the desk and took out his stethoscope and blood pressure cuff. "Let's take a look at that head of yours, Frank." He turned Gramps' head to get a better look. "Hmmm, I think you need a trip to the hospital. You need your head examined, in more ways than one. Probably need a couple of stitches, too."

"Ain't gonna happen," Gramps answered defiantly.

Doc listened to his heart and took his blood pressure, "Pressure's high, but that's to be expected, and your heart is dancing a conga. Let's just put you in for the night."

"I don't need no damn hospital. Give me a couple of aspirin and leave me alone," the older man shouted. "Ow, not a good idea," he added— holding his head in his hands.

"Stubborn ol' fool. Nora, you can take him home, but watch him. Wake him every couple of hours. He's got a slight concussion. Too bad he wasn't hit harder. Then maybe I could shove him into the hospital for a proper checkup. Did you ever have that appointment booked for the checkup at Manatee Memorial like I asked?" he queried Nora.

"Yes, Nurse Hill called me. He has the appointment in two weeks. He wouldn't go until the picking was finished. I'm taking him myself, so he can't back out of it."

"Good, I want to see those results." Doc packed his bag and shook hands with Gabe. He tipped his hat at Nora, looked at Gramps mumbling, "Stubborn," and called his service to let them know he was leaving the Hollister place and walked out to his car.

Gabe and Nora helped Gramps down to his jeep. Nora drove, and Gabe followed them back to the house. They helped him get settled on the couch. Nora tried to put an afghan over him and left some water within his reach. He complained about all the fuss, refusing to go to his bed. "I'm fine. It will take more than a bump on the head to send me to my bed like an invalid."

They left the old man, the dog at his side, and went to the kitchen.

"How about a cup of tea, or would you prefer something cold," Nora offered.

"You got any more of those beers in the fridge?" Gabe asked.

"Good idea, I'll take one, too. We can sit on the porch." Nora grabbed two cold ones from the fridge and led the way. Flashing lights from a couple of police cars cast a kaleidoscope of blue and red in the night sky down by the packing plant.

"I called in the forensic team to go over the office. You never know. Maybe they'll find something. Hopefully fingerprints," Gabe said.

"Who could have done this? Everyone loves Gramps, and he's always fair with everyone."

Gabe took a sip, patting Hobo's head as she took up residence in his lap. "There is one person who has a reason to be mad at your grandfather."

"You mean Tito," Nora answered.

"Yeah, Tito. I think I'll have my men find him and bring him in." Gabe finished his beer, placed the reluctant cat in his lap onto the floor, and stood. "I'd like to stay, but even though I'm technically off duty, I want to chase this down. I'll drop by later tomorrow and check up on Gramps—and you, of course."

Nora stood and looked at the lights by the plant and then at Gabe. "I know you have to go, but I like you, uh, here with me on the porch."

"I like it, too," Gabe said. He took Nora by the shoulders and drew her closer to him. He tilted his head and gently kissed her lips. He couldn't help himself and deepened the kiss and felt her responding. She slipped her arms around his neck, holding onto him and resting her head on his shoulder long after the kiss ended. Kissing him brought to life sensations deep within her.

"You're lucky we have a chaperone. Even if he is snoring away on the couch," Gabe said, taking a breath and pushing Nora back to arm's length. In the dim light, he could still see the awakening desire in her eyes.

"I really have to go," he said with regret. "And you need to keep checking on Gramps. I also have Dan at my place. I'll come by tomorrow."

Nora walked Gabe out past her grandfather on the couch. "Night, Gabe," Gramps said. They both laughed and walked hand-in-hand to Gabe's car.

Gabe was in his office, nursing his second cup of over-brewed coffee when Sgt. Alvarez came knocking on his door. He signaled for the sergeant to come in.

"What have you got?" Gabe asked wearily. He had gotten practically no sleep after leaving Nora's porch. Not only the events of last night had him riled up, but his thoughts also kept running off track and back to Nora.

"We got some fingerprints from the desk in that office. One of them matched a ten card right back to a recent guest of ours, Tito Ramirez."

"Good work; go pick him up. I want him in here today," Gabe said. "I'm meeting Dan for an early

lunch, and then I'm going to check-on Frank Hollister. Call me when you find Ramirez."
Dan was already at the small diner when Gabe walked in. He waved him over to his booth in the back where they could talk and not be overheard. Gabe slid in, taking off his hat and sun glasses.

"Boy, do you look rough," Dan said—noticing the weary look in Gabe's eyes.

"Yeah, yeah," he said signaling for the waitress to bring over more coffee. "Right now, the only thing keeping me upright is coffee."

"You said you had a suspect?" Dan prompted.

"Tito Ramirez." Gabe proceeded to fill Dan in on how Ramirez had worked for Hollister and got fired for falsifying records. Then he told him how Richie had gotten him bailed out.

"There are connections here," Gabe continued. "But I can't get a handle on how it all fits yet. There are still some pieces missing. That plane showed up right when Richie and Tito got bailed out. Then on the next run, Richie turns up dead. I don't figure Tito for a killer, but he's connected somehow. I just have to figure it out."

The waitress came over, refilled their cups, and took an order for two burgers and fries.

After she left, Dan said, "I might be able to help you out a bit. I called D.C. this morning and talked to my office. Word is going around that your area is the prime location for the cartels and their cocaine drops. The Medellin Cartel is the biggest there is, and they're making a move into central Florida. Now, just what if, the plane you and Nora witnessed is dropping cocaine? Someone has to pick it up. Let's say this Richie and Tito get hired to do that pick up. What we don't know is who killed Richie and why."

Dan tucked into his burger, "Say, this is pretty good," he said around a mouthful and signaled the waitress for more coffee. "Can I get a piece of that blueberry pie, too?"

"Sure can, honey," she said giving him a quick wink.

"Ok quit flirting with Doris and get back on track," Gabe shook his head. *"Same ol' Dan."*

"We're back to last night and who robbed the packing plant. Who would know that the pay packets would be handed out on Friday?" Gabe asked eating more of his burger, following it with a bit of coffee to wash it down.

"And who would know about the Jessup place? An old man all by himself, an empty field, a back way in-and-out . . .?" Dan continued the thought as the two men ate their burgers in silence for a few minutes. "Who knew all these things, yet is no more than a stupid patsy?" Dan asked around a mouthful of burger—catsup on his chin.

"Tito Ramirez," they said at the same time.

"Doris," Dan called. "Make that pie to go."

Dan grabbed the check from the table, "I've got an expense account," he explained. Gabe left the tip, and they hurried to get back to the station.

Reaching the station, Gabe yelled for Sgt. Alvarez, "You get a bead on Tito Ramirez yet?"

Alvarez was getting ready to go out. Putting on a flak jacket, he took an assault rifle off the rack and shouted back, "Yeah, he's at a low-rate motel out by the highway in Bradenton. I was just taking a squad out to round him up."

"Good, we'll follow you out. I want him in one piece. He's got a lot of the answers to what's been going on around here."

Dan and Gabe hurried back to Gabe's patrol car and joined the other cars on the way to pick up Tito.

"If Tito is involved with the cartel and the cocaine drops, he must know he's in way over his head," Gabe said.

"If by any chance, he was there when Cantura was killed, he's already in deep," Dan added.

"Tito's in big trouble," Gabe said.

Dan agreed. "He knows way too much to be left running around loose."

Chapter Twelve

It took almost an hour to get out to Bradenton and the motel. Gabe had the patrol cars stay out of sight until he could talk to the manager and find out which room Tito was in.

The manager's office was near the front. Gabe walked in and didn't see anyone at the desk, but he could hear a game show playing on a television in the back. He rang a bell on the counter and called out, "Sheriff's Office. Anyone here?"

A seedy-looking man emerged from the back with a cigarette hanging out of the corner of his mouth. He wore a rumpled t-shirt and jeans that looked like he had slept in them for days. A shower and shave were missing, too. Gabe could smell him from across the counter. A mixture of stale sweat, old booze and cigarette smoke had him trying not to breathe too deeply.

"I'm looking for this man," Gabe said, showing him a mug shot of Tito Ramirez.

"Yeah, he's here. What you want him for?" the man asked. Working the smoking cigarette around in his mouth, he tossed the picture back across the counter to Gabe.

"He needs to answer some questions for us. What's his room number?"

"Number nine, this building, last room on the bottom."

"Thanks," Gabe said—picking up the photo and warning, "Stay away from the phone and stay inside."

The clerk walked back to his television, "None of my business anyway," he grumbled.

The motel had three buildings arranged in a horseshoe fashion with a second-floor walkway connecting them. Some officers went to the room next to Tito's, knocked on the door softly, and had the occupants—a young couple with a baby—moved out of harm's way just in case things went sideways. Gabe told his men to go around the back and come in between the two buildings, staying low and away from the windows. He wasn't sure what Tito Ramirez was capable of, or if he had any weapons.

Gabe and Dan, wearing flak jackets, walked up to the door of room nine. Standing to the side of the door, Gabe had his gun out ready and knocked hard. "Tito Ramirez, this is Sheriff McAlister. Open the door and come out here. We need to talk."

The men could feel the tension in the air. The curtains in the window above the ancient leaky air conditioner moved. The door cracked open, and Tito peeked out.

"Who's that with you?" he asked.

"This is Dan Parker. He's with the DEA in Washington."

"What's that?"

Dan took a chance and stepped out where Tito could see him better. "The DEA is the Drug Enforcement Agency. We're like the police or sheriff here except we only deal with drugs and the people that are bringing them into the country. I think you might have gotten mixed up with some very bad guys here, Tito."

Both Dan and Gabe could see the wheels turning in Tito's head. There was no place to run. He was not a stupid person. Just some of his choices were. "Okay, I'm coming out." Gabe signaled for his men to stay back.

"Come out with your hands up," Gabe instructed. "We don't want anyone to get hurt." Tito eased the door open and stepped out, hands in the air.

Sergeant Alvarez came up with two more officers. They tossed Tito up against the building and searched him for weapons. One of them grabbed his hands and pulled them behind his back, putting cuffs on him.

"Take him to the station and sit on him until I get there," Gabe said. "He doesn't talk to anyone except me or Dan. No phone calls either, at least not yet." Alvarez marched Tito to a squad car while reading him his rights and deposited him in the back seat, not too gently.

Gabe walked into the motel room and found the empty pay packets tossed over the bed and floor. The money was in a neat pile on the dresser along with a half-empty bottle of cheap tequila and the remains of a take-out pizza.

"Well that went better than expected," Dan said.

"Yeah, I think he knows he's better off with us than with the cartel."

Back at the station, Tito was put in an interrogation room to wait for Dan and Gabe. He paced the room nervously back and forth, running his fingers through his hair. Through the intercom, they could hear him talking to himself as he walked. "Oh, shit. Oh, shit. I'm in for it now. If I get out of this, I'm a dead man. If I go to prison, I'm a dead man. Oh, shit. Shit fuckin' damn. I really screwed up bad this time."

Gabe felt sorry for the guy. Tito was a pawn in a much bigger game. Dan wanted to grill him hard, though, for information on the Medellin Cartel.

"I think he's stewed long enough," Gabe said. "Let's see what he knows."

Dan followed Gabe in, and they sat down at a scarred wooden table in the middle of the room. Tito took a seat on the other side, "Thanks for the water, Sheriff," he said taking a drink from the bottle Gabe handed him. "Cheap tequila gives me a right bad head. Look man, you got me," he finally blurted out.

"What exactly did you do, Tito?" Gabe asked, nice and friendly like.

"Don't give me that, Sheriff. You know I stole that money from Hollister's. Is the old man okay? He wasn't supposed to be there. I just wanted the money. No one was supposed to get hurt. When I saw the dog, I freaked. Hollister was not supposed to be there. I swear I didn't want to hurt the guy, but I had to have that money. I'm in a hell of a mess." Tito was talking fast, shaking nervously and scared out of his mind.

"Mr. Hollister sustained a mild concussion and will be fine. We recovered all the stolen money, so the workers can be paid and move on."

Tito seemed to relax a tiny bit on hearing this.

Dan took over asking, "Did you mean to kill Mr. Jessup, or was that not supposed to happen either?"

"What?" Tito jumped up. "That wasn't me! I didn't touch that man!" He was pacing the room again—back and forth, wall to wall, across the table from Dan and Gabe.

"So, you were there that night?"Dan asked.

"This is bad; this is so bad," Tito said as he walked. "Okay, I was there. But Mr. Jessup is old and deaf. He was supposed to stay in the house, asleep."

"I think you'd better tell us the whole story, Tito. Why were you and whoever was with you there in the first place?" Dan asked.

"I can't tell you anything. They'll kill me if I talk to you guys."

"Who's going to kill you? You have to give me names."

"No way. Those guys have a pretty far reach."

Gabe stood up and said, "Okay, you can go to prison for robbery and attempted murder. I'm sure your friends will love to have you in a nice cozy cell where anything can happen."

Tito sat back down at the table and dropped his head into his hands. "Jesus, I'm so screwed."

"We can help you—maybe even offer witness protection." Dan said. "You give us useful information, agree to testify against these friends you're so afraid of, and we give you a new life, new name and no jail time." Dan had the power to offer this to Tito, if and only if he cooperated with the DEA.

"How do I know you can do that?"

"How do you know I can't?" Dan asked. "I can and I will if you give me what I need to get the guys responsible."

"Tito, I want the guy who killed Mr. Jessup and Richie Cantura," Gabe said.

"And I want the people who are in that plane dropping cocaine in Florida," Dan said. "The DEA is going after the Medellin Cartel, with or without your help. But I'm the only one who can give you witness protection and a new identity."

"You guys really know how to team up against a person," Tito said. He lifted his head and looked over at Gabe and Dan. "Do you promise I get this witness protection thing?"

"You have my word," Dan said, making the sign of the cross over his heart and raising his hand.

This Tito understood. "The guy's name is Santos. That's all I know him by."

"That's a start," Dan said.

Chapter Thirteen

For the next couple of hours Tito answered questions. Gabe knew that it had started with Richie Cantura helping to bail out Tito.

"Who put up the bail money for you and Richie?" Gabe asked.

"I thought Santos did," Tito answered.

"When did you first meet this guy, Santos?" Gabe asked.

"He was waiting for us when we walked out of jail that morning. We got in a van, and he took us to an abandoned tool shop."

Dan took over the questioning for a while when Gabe stepped out to have Alvarez run down who had put up the bail money. Maybe it was Santos, but he wanted to be sure there was not another player he needed to know about.

"Call down to Jenny on the desk and ask her to look up whose name is on the bail release for Tito Ramirez and Richie Cantura."

Gabe needed to call Nora, too, and tell her they had Tito in custody and all the money had been recovered. He should have called as soon as they got back to the station, but things had moved so fast he forgot.

He closed the door in his office to make the call. He was nervous as he dialed Nora's number. He wanted to tell her about Tito but so much more.

The phone rang several times, and he was about to give up when someone finally picked it up.

"Hello," Nora said.

"A . . . hi, Nora, this is Gabe," he stuttered.

"Oh, Gabe, we've been so worried. Tell me what happened. Did you find Tito? Was anyone hurt?"

"We arrested Tito, and no one got hurt. He's in with Dan right now. I'm afraid he's gotten himself into a bit of a mess."

She hesitated and asked hopefully, "Can you come over?"

"Not tonight. I want to, but it's been a long day, and I have a pile of paperwork to do over this. I want to hang around and see what Dan finds out. Tito admitted to the robbery and hitting your grandfather. He didn't think your Gramps would be there.

"We know he set up going over to the Jessup's place. But Jessup was supposed to be asleep. How Tito figured flying a plane in-and-out and the noise of it almost landing wouldn't wake him up I can't fathom. Even if Jessup was deaf, the vibrations would have had him looking."

"When can we have the money back for the workers? Gramps wants to know what to tell them," Nora said, a deep concern for Gramps and their workers in her voice.

"Tell Gramps I'll bring it by tomorrow. I'll even help stuff the packets. Maybe we can hand out the money after mass on Sunday. But I don't know when exactly I'll be there. It all depends on what we find out today."

Gabe had started walking around his desk, but the cord from the telephone would only let him go so far. He untangled it and went in the opposite direction only to get stuck again.

"Why don't you and Dan come over for supper tomorrow about six? We can work on the packets after that," Nora suggested, doing her own tour of the kitchen as far as her cord would reach.

"Do I have to bring Dan?" Gabe asked, joking.

"He doesn't have to come if he has other plans, but you should ask him," Nora said.

"I'll see you tomorrow then," Gabe said hoping nothing would get in the way of his seeing her again.

"Yeah, tomorrow, bye," Nora hung up first and leaned against the kitchen counter. She hoped Dan would have other plans but quickly felt guilty for the thought.

Gabe put the phone back in its cradle. He sat down at his desk and leaned back, fingers crossed that Dan would have other plans for tomorrow night. He didn't want to share his time with Nora.

Dan came busting in the door, "Grab your hat. We got to go."

Startled, Gabe stood. "Where are we going?" he called as he grabbed his hat off the rack and hurried to catch up with Dan.

Dan bounced into the passenger seat, and Gabe got behind the wheel.

"If I'm driving, I need to know where we're going," Gabe said.

"Head out to West Oak Road on the way to Arcadia. Tito said there was an old abandoned garage or tool shop before the spot where the road divides. He said it was blue with a tin roof and real rusty looking."

Starting the engine, they headed off toward West Oak Road. Traffic was light. They made good time. Most folks were already home for the night. Ranchers were the early-to-bed and early-to-rise type. Only Main Street would have any business at night.

A half hour later, Dan called out, "There, on the right!" There were no cars near the building, and the lights inside were off. Gabe pulled into a vacant lot a fair distance away, and the two men got out and closed the patrol car's doors softly, just in case.

Gabe went to the trunk and took out a couple of flashlights and two flak jackets. He handed one of each to Dan. "Just in case," he said.

They found a break in the chain link fence that surrounded the sides and back of the property. Squeezing through, they made their way around to the back of the building.

The ground was uneven, covered with broken bottles and empty cans hiding in the tall grass, waiting to trip someone. "If I break an ankle in this, I'm sending the DEA the bill," Gabe moaned.

The windows were too dirty to see inside, but the flickering glow of a television was visible. Dan looked at Gabe and shrugged, "Someone's home."

They kept low, walking to find a way in. Finally, they found one—around the front there was a door with a brand-new Yale lock set in the old door.

"Someone is using the building," Gabe said. "Question is who."

Gabe tried the door and found it locked. Dan nudged Gabe out of his way. "Let me at that lock." He took a small case out of his pocket. Gabe watched as Dan unzipped the case and produced a small set of tools for picking locks.

"You're a man of many talents, Dan," Gabe whispered.

"That I am. Just watch, and keep an eye out."

In seconds, Dan had the lock picked and the door open. Turning off their flashlights, they opened the door slowly the rest of the way and carefully walked in.

The place was old and smelled of oil and grease. The worn sign above the door read, "Foster and Son Welding," which made sense with the welding equipment and benches around the room.

Someone was asleep in front of the television— his head lolling back, snoring away with an AK-47 assault rifle lying across his lap. An empty pizza box and liter of coke sat on a table nearby.

Dan motioned for Gabe to be quiet while he cautiously stepped over and took the rifle from the sleeping man.

"This is too easy," Dan joked. Gabe had to suppress a laugh. He placed the muzzle of the rifle to the man's chest and gave him a hard poke. The man muttered and shifted position slightly. Dan poked him again.

This time the man woke up fast and confused. "Hey, what's going on here? Who the hell are you guys?"

Gabe identified himself, "Sheriff McAlister."

"I'm Dan Parker from the DEA, and you, my man, are going to answer some questions for us down at the station."

Gabe slapped cuffs on him and spun him around, "Let's start with your name first."

The man acted defiant and then thought better of it under his present circumstances. "Name's Manny," he said, confused and not completely awake.

"How about the name your mother gave you, smart ass?" Dan said—shoving the man hard in the shoulder and forcing him to sit back hard in his chair.

"Okay, okay, 'Manuel Hernandez.' Are you happy now?"

"Be even happier when you're in a cell," Dan growled close to his face. "Stay put, and don't move an inch." Gabe pulled out his cuffs and secured Manuel to the chair.

Shining a light around, they found that one of the benches by the back wall had been recently used. All the rest were covered in dust, animal tracks and mouse or rat droppings.

"Hey, look at this," Dan called, holding up a scale. Another smaller one was nearby.

"I've got some torn black plastic wrap over here. There's white powdery stuff on the inside." Gabe pointed to a pile on the floor. He also found gallon-size clear bags.

At the end of the bench, there was a large locked cabinet. Gabe tried the lock, but it was a combination lock and couldn't be picked by Dan. They would need bolt cutters to get into the cabinet.

"You know, I don't know a lot about how they move their drugs. I'm guessing it's pretty much the same as marijuana."

"Yeah, pretty much, Dan explained."They break down the packages that are dropped from the plane into smaller units—each one weighing the same. Once the next dealer gets his portion, he cuts the cocaine with whatever to make it go further and repackages it in even smaller amounts."

"What kind of stuff do they use to cut it with?" Gabe asked. He had been in law enforcement for several years now, but he had a lot to learn about the drug trafficking coming into his area.

"Whatever they have handy—could be powdered milk, corn starch, some even use sugar or ground drywall, anything that looks the same as the cocaine. People get killed just by what the cocaine has been cut with to make it go further and increase the dealers' profit," Dan explained.

"It makes me mad that the dealers have no concern for human life. All they want is money. By the time it hits the street, it's been handled several times. Judging by those black wrappers over there, the street value of this stuff is way in excess of several million.

"We've found where they repackage the cocaine for distribution to the first set of dealers. Whoever it is most likely has a notebook with who gets how much and what they pay. If we could get that book, we could shut down a big part of the cartel's operation," Dan said.

"Leave everything as it is. We've got to take this guy with us. Maybe they'll think he just gave up and left. I don't want to let them know we were here, or they'll move the operation, and we might not get another chance like this."

"Agreed," Gabe said.

They went out the way they had come in. Back at the patrol car, Manuel was shoved into the back seat. "Hey, you guys can't grab me up for no reason," Manuel shouted.

Dan turned and again flashed his badge in the man's face, "This says I can."

"I got rights you know," Manuel tried again.

"Your rights are what I say they are. Right now, you have the right to shut the hell up or ride in the trunk."

After a bit of silence, Gabe said, "I've got to remember that trick."

"Works every time," Dan laughed. "I've got to call Washington and get some agents down here. We need to find out how they're getting it distributed. I don't suppose Tito would be up for a little undercover work and wearing a wire?"

"Right now, he's afraid of his own shadow. But given the right incentive, he might be talked into it," Gabe said—willing to try anything.

As he drove, Gabe asked, "You're really into taking these guys down. Any particular reason? I've always wondered why you went to the DEA after the FBI."

"You remember my cousin, Jeff? You met him a couple of times when he came to visit me in college."

"Yeah, I remember him," Gabe nodded, waiting for Dan to fill the silence.

"He got into marijuana and eventually found his way to cocaine. He was like a brother to me growing up. You know I didn't have any siblings. He was as close as I got. While I was in college, I couldn't keep an eye on him, and he slid down the drug road. After college, he didn't even make it to my graduation. I lost track of him.

I was about a year into the FBI when my mom called and told me he had overdosed on cocaine. They found him in a fleabag hotel. He'd been dead four days. The only reason they found him was the manager investigated the smell. That's why the DEA and why I hate the dealers that do this just for the money."

The men were quiet for a while. Gabe understood Dan's motives. Law enforcement drew men for all sorts of reasons.

"Hey, man, I can understand how you feel. I liked Jeff, too." Gabe said. His stomach suddenly rumbled—reminding him they hadn't eaten in a while. "Any chance of something to eat? Maybe swing into a burger joint?"

"Sure. We'll stop at a drive thru," Dan offered.

"Hey! What about me? I could use a burger, too, guys," Manuel complained.

"Yeah, you too," Gabe replied.

"Gabe, when we get to the station, I want some time alone with this guy."

"Dan, ol' Buddy, I don't think that's gonna happen. I understand you wanting to mess him up, but I can't allow that. It's my station, so I'll do it," Gabe said loudly.

Manuel let loose a string of expletives about police harassment and no one reading him his rights. By the time they reached the parking lot, he was hollering for a lawyer, while trying to stuff the rest of his burger in his mouth. Dan had come up with the idea of cuffing one hand to the car door so Manuel could eat.

Back in the station, Manuel was put in a cell to consider his choices. Dan and Gabe talked about how they could convince Tito to cooperate and how to set it up.

Dan called his headquarters in D.C. and got the ball rolling to send down some men to back them up. They would arrive tomorrow afternoon or the next day. Dan would have to find some rooms for them while they were here.

Gabe sat as his desk, leaning back in his chair, "I forgot to tell you that Nora asked both of us to supper tomorrow night," he said.

"The lovely Nora, eh?" Dan replied. "Have you decided to stake a claim or not?"

"I never thought much about settling down, but now. . ."

"Take my advice and stake that claim because honestly, I'm surprised someone hasn't snapped her up already. If I thought I could stand the heat and humidity down here, I'd transfer in a minute and take her myself. But from what I've seen, she's already made up her mind, and I think you have, too. You just don't know what to do about it," Dan stood up laughing.

"I'm heading back to your place. I'll pick up some groceries for us on the way. No offense, but your spaghetti routine is getting a bit boring."

"What about some steaks on that expense account of yours?" Gabe had to laugh himself. He really needed to buy himself a cookbook and learn to fix something that didn't come out of a box or a jar.

He debated about calling Nora. It was almost ten o'clock by now, but he lost the debate and dialed . . . and waited.

Gramps answered, "Hello."

"Hi Gramps, I suppose Nora is in bed asleep already?"

"No, she's out on the porch. Do you want me to get her for you?"

"Please, I wanted to tell her how today went. We found where they are bringing the cocaine. Do you remember a place called Foster's and Son Welding?"

"Sure, I do. He used to fix farm equipment. Did good work, too. His son was killed in Viet Nam. He lost interest in the business after that, and it only lasted a few more years. It went downhill, and he finally gave it up. I think he moved out of the area, up north somewhere I think. He had a daughter in Virginia, I believe."

"Thanks, Gramps. Can I talk to Nora now?"

"Oh, right. I'll go get her for you."

Gabe waited a few minutes before she finally came on the line. "Hi, Gabe."

"Hi there. Sorry for calling so late."

"That's okay. I was on the porch, hoping I might see that plane again."

"If you do, just call me. Don't even think about chasing it yourself. Those men are dangerous. Dan is calling up to D.C. to get some of his agents down here to help. We found where they are bringing the cocaine. We're going to set up a sting operation.

You know, stake out the building. Wait for them to come back."

"Gabe, they might not come back to the same place. If they have all the cocaine, won't they try to ship it out as soon as possible?"

"Right, but we have to find out how and where from. We thought we might use Tito. Set him up with a wire and have him talk to this guy Santos. He seems to be in charge. I'm willing to bet he's just the muscle. There has to be a brain in all this somewhere."

"Do you think Tito will help you out and wear a wire? That's very dangerous for him. He could get killed." Nora was worried for Tito. He might not be able to pull something like this off.

"I hope he goes along with it. It's about the only shot we have right now."

Gabe and Nora talked for a bit but mostly just listened to the other breathe. They both had lots to say but didn't know how to say it. Finally, Nora asked if Gabe was going to the dance at the fire station at the end of the month.

"It's the last dance before the summer gets too hot," Nora said.

"Well, I guess it would be my civic duty to attend."

"I don't suppose you have a pretty girl in mind."

"It's the first I've heard about it," Gabe confessed. "Could I coax you into being my date for the evening?"

"Gee, I don't know," Nora giggled. "I'll have to think about it and let you know."

"I hope we have these drug smugglers in jail by then," he said getting serious again.

"Me, too. I don't like the idea of these guys running around. The whole thing scares me a bit."

"Does that offer for dinner tomorrow night still stand?" Gabe asked. "I broke down and asked Dan, and he said he'd like to come."

"Sure, how's six o'clock sound?" Nora did a little school girl dance at the thought of seeing Gabe again.

"Sounds good," Gabe said smiling to himself. "Well, you don't go doing anything foolish, and I'll see you tomorrow night."

"See you tomorrow," Nora sighed and hung up the phone.

Chapter Fourteen

The following evening, Nora bustled around the kitchen table. She reset the dishes on the table several times, rearranging the silverware, repositioning the glasses.

"Chica, don't fuss so much. Men don't even notice the table. So long as there is plenty of food, they will be happy." Rosita stirred the yellow rice on the stove. Nora got in her way to open the oven and check the chicken pieces—roasting away smothered in red peppers, onions, and mushrooms, swimming in Rosita's secret seasonings.

"You are driving me crazy. Go outside and worry in the driveway. There is only so much room in this kitchen," Rosita laughed as Nora threw a dish towel on the counter and stormed out.

Nora was a barrel of nerves, sitting on the back steps waiting, her toes tapping. She was not good at waiting at the best of times. Her mind kept going over all the things that could go wrong. Was Gabe allergic to the spices in her chicken? Maybe he hated chicken. Would he like her cooking? Would he like the dress she had on? Did she put on too much perfume? A million questions danced through her head. Dan was coming, too, but her thoughts were only on Gabe.

She saw headlights turn off the main road and head up to her house. Show time, she thought. She crossed her fingers and sent a wish to the evening star that everything would go smoothly tonight.

Dust swirled around as Gabe brought the patrol car to a stop in the driveway. Both men got out and walked her way.

Nora blushed when Dan complimented her. "You look nice tonight, Nora," Dan said. She had spent extra time getting ready. She didn't own many dresses and had picked out a sensible yellow shirtwaist to wear and a decent pair of shoes instead of her tried and true cowboy boots.

"Yeah, real nice," Gabe said—handing her a bottle of wine he had picked up. "Hope it will go with whatever we're having."

Nora read the label. "This will be perfect," she said about the Merlot he had chosen. She really didn't know much about wine and winged it.

Gramps opened the screen door and called, "Come on in here, guys. Food will get cold, and I'm starved."

Rosita placed the food on the table and then left for her own supper with Hector. Her nephew, Mateo, had turned up on her doorstep unexpectedly a few weeks ago. He was supposed to be looking for work, but most of his days were about sleeping after being out all night.

Walking in the door to her small house, Rosita saw Mateo lounging in front of the television. Hector saw her and looking at her nephew, shrugging his shoulders.

Her sister, Juanita, still lived in Columbia, and she had not seen her since coming to the states. That seemed like a world away. They wrote back and forth and sent pictures. Every year, the sisters planned to visit each other, but it never happened. Juanita wrote about the hardships in Columbia with Pablo Escobar and the cartel trying to take over the government. She wrote that she had heard the cartel had blown up the police station—killing many.

Rosita had tried to talk to her nephew several times about why he was here. All his answers had been very evasive and gave away nothing. She wanted to help him and her sister, but she had to make him get a proper job or else . . . ."

"Hello, Mateo, any luck finding work today? Did you go to the orange juice factory in Bradenton? They usually have work, especially right after the harvest is finished."

He didn't even answer Rosita. He got up, grabbed a jacket and left, slamming the door behind him.

"Hector, I am so sorry. I don't know what to do," she cried, tears in her eyes. She was hurt and embarrassed by her nephew's actions.

Hector came and embraced her tightly, "Do not worry. Things have a way of working themselves out. On Sunday, we will pray again for God to find a way to help us."

Gramps took his usual place at the head of the table and invited his guests to take a seat. "We're happy you could make it tonight. I thought maybe the bad guys would have you working this evening."

"No chasing bad guys tonight. We took the night off," Dan said.

"This looks wonderful, Nora. I don't often get a home-cooked meal," Gabe said.

"Yeah. His specialty is spaghetti and sauce from a jar," Dan offered.

"Nothing wrong with that. Now dig in and pass the cornbread," Gramps said taking a piece of chicken onto his plate and passing the rest along the table.

"I hope everything is okay. Rosita usually does the cooking. She gave me a couple of her recipes to try," Nora said, anxiously waiting for her guests to take their first bite. "She has a nephew visiting. Maybe you'd like to meet him sometime?"

"Sure, Nora, if we get the time with all that is going on right now," Gabe said. "This is really good, Nora. Thanks for inviting us," he added, spreading butter on his piece of warm cornbread. The men tucked into the rich dish of chicken sautéed with peppers, onions and spices served over yellow rice to catch the hearty sauce.

Dan could only nod his agreement, his mouth full. Taking a sip of wine, he said, "Nora, if you cook like this every night, I'll marry you tomorrow."

"No way, I saw her first," Gabe found himself saying.

"Two worthy suitors, Nora," Gramps laughed. "They do say the way to a man's heart is through his stomach."

Nora flushed with embarrassment, changing the subject quickly. "What is happening with finding out who's behind all this drug business?" she asked.

"I've asked the DEA to send me some agents from Washington. They should arrive in the morning," Dan said.

"We have a man in custody that was supposed to be guarding their place of operations," Gabe said. "We've been talking to him all day, but he's not telling us anything we don't already know. Dan and I have been working on Tito to wear a wire. He's so afraid of his own shadow that he still won't agree to do it."

"I don't blame him, but what if I talked to him?" Nora surprised them by her offer. "He used to work for us. Maybe I could convince him to do it. But then again, maybe it's not such a good idea. We did get him arrested after all."

"I don't want you involved, Nora," Gabe said. Gramps stopped his fork halfway to his mouth. Noticing Gabe was a little protective of his granddaughter, he smiled.

"Me either, but we might have to give it a try. It can't hurt," Dan ventured.

"I don't like it, Nora," Gramps said—pushing away his empty plate.

"We don't have to decide tonight. We can see what the agents from D.C. have to say and go from there," Dan said.

"Right. How about having coffee and key lime pie on the porch?" Nora suggested as she stood up and started to clear off the table. Gabe and Dan both stood to help her. "Oh, no you don't," Nora said —taking some dishes from Dan. "You're both guests tonight. Next time, I'll have you do the washing up. Go on the porch and talk to Gramps. I'll be along in a minute."

Puttering around the kitchen, clearing the table and getting the coffee and pie ready, she thought of Tito wearing a wire. She just didn't think he could pull it off and hoped he wouldn't have to. There had to be another way to track where the shipment went from the shop in Arcadia and where they were keeping the plane. If she couldn't help with Tito, maybe she could help locate the plane.

After clearing up in the kitchen, Nora joined the men on the porch. "So, what is the big discussion out here? Are you educating them on growing oranges in Florida or catching bad guys, Gramps?"

Gabe jumped up to help her place the coffee and pie on a table. Dan and Gabe helped themselves, juggling the cups and plates. Nora had to boot Hobo out of his favorite chair to sit down. The cat wound himself around her legs, tail in the air.

"He's telling me it's his dinner time, too," Nora said. "I'll get to you in a minute."

After dessert, Gabe insisted on helping Nora take the dishes to the kitchen. He leaned against the counter, watching her while she fed the cat.

"Come take a walk with me," Gabe took her hand and guided her out the back door.

"What about Dan? We can't just leave him," Nora protested.

"Yes, we can. Your gramps is on the porch with him, and didn't you notice? Dan was closing his eyes. He'll be asleep and not even notice we're gone. It's been a rough few days, and we're all exhausted."

"And you're not?" Nora asked—her eyes wide with question.

"Not too tired to be with you."

They walked in the direction of the stable hand-in-hand. The evening was warm but with a cool sea breeze coming from the west.

Ending up in the barn, arms resting on the door to Jasper's stable, they stared into each other's eyes. "You must have brought me out here for something, Gabe," she said smiling knowingly.

"Yeah, I did," Gabe took her arms from the door and turned her towards him. He gently kissed her. Not satisfied with one, he went back for more. She tasted sweet and warmed his heart. They both could feel the desire for more than kisses, and the hayloft above called to them. Breaking away, breathless, hearts pounding, they stood their ground.

"We can't," Nora said, staring at the ground. Gabe shifted, uncomfortable, not sure what to do. He wanted her in the worst way.

"You're right," he stammered. "Nora, you must know how I feel about you, and I think you feel the same about me." He took her hands again and brought them to his lips and kissed her palms one-by-one. She felt her insides churning with emotions she had never felt before—desires she was trying not to think about.

"Will you be my girl and see where it leads us?" he asked.

"On one condition," she said.

"What's that?" he asked, a puzzled look on his face, not sure he wanted the answer.

"You let me teach you to ride," she giggled.

"Deal," he answered. He wasn't sure what he had just gotten himself in to. He was a city kid, after all.

"Deal," they laughed, shaking hands.

Jasper let out a loud whinny as if he understood, too, tossing his head up and down in approval.

They walked back to the house, stopping outside the door for one more kiss. When they stepped out to the porch, Gramps smiled, "Well, if you two don't look like the cat that ate the canary."

Dan roused himself, stood up and grabbed Gabe's hand. "It's about time you made a decision, old man. Guess I'll have to console myself with beer and cheap women."

The group sat around the kitchen table and helped Gramps fill the pay packets to hand out the next day after morning Mass.

Chapter Fifteen

Gabe and Dan met with the DEA agents from Washington at the Tampa Airport. There were three men and one woman. Agent Maggie O'Donnell was the senior agent. Agents Montrose, Baker and Esposito all had skills and training in drug enforcement.

When Dan saw the agents in baggage claim at the airport, he had whispered in Gabe's ear, "Here comes trouble." He explained that Montrose and O'Donnell didn't get along that well. O'Donnell was a hard-working female and was rising fast through the ranks. Montrose was old school and resented O'Donnell and her success. He was lazy and hard to work with. Baker and Esposito, he didn't know that much about. They were both young, eager and out to make a name for themselves.

Once back at the station, the agents and Gabe discussed strategies, trying to find ways to bring this arm of the cartel down. Gabe's men had been sitting on the tool shop in Arcadia, reporting in every couple of hours. No one had been seen there since the night they surprised and apprehended Manuel, aka Manny Hernandez.

"So far, the only name we have is Santos. We don't think that's his real name, but he could be running the operation. Someone is flying the plane, and someone is giving the orders. I don't think they are both the same person, either. Why pick the old tool shop to distribute the drugs? They had to know that it was abandoned. Who knows all this stuff?"

"Have there been any strangers around asking questions?" Agent O'Donnell asked.

"Not that I know of. The migrant workers have moved on to their next crop. The majority left after getting paid this morning after Mass. The rest will follow over the next couple of days," Gabe said. "I've been talking to Mr. Hollister, and he never mentioned any of them staying around.

"Has there been any movement at the tool shop?" Agent Esposito asked.

"We've had an officer watching the place, but so far nothing. I don't think they'll be going back there," Dan said.

Agent O'Donnell went over and poured herself another cup of coffee. "Yech! This tastes like old socks. Don't you guys have a decent coffee shop around here?"

"There's only one coffee shop around here," Gabe said trying to stop laughing at her distress. "The 'By the Slice Diner' in town. They do a great cup of coffee." The stress and tension were getting to them. A little laughter helped to relieve it.

"Burgers too," added Dan. "And don't forget the blueberry pie."

"Okay, wise guys," she said pouring the coffee in the sink. "You're a couple of comedians."

Montrose spoke up and said, "Why don't you make a pot. You seem to be the only one complaining."

O'Donnell held her tongue and glared at him. She had put up with his remarks on the plane from D.C. She wanted to get this job over with. She walked over to the water cooler, filled a paper cup with water and returned to the table.

"Where around here can a small plane take off and land without arousing suspicion?" Agent O'Donnell asked.

"There's a small airport right to the south east of Arcadia," Gabe said. "They could use that or just about any large pasture in the county would do. There are acres of land out here that no one ever uses except for cattle. There are roads in and out of the groves where a plane could land. We have to get our eyes on that plane again and try and track it somehow."

"The how is the hard part," Agent Montrose said. "What about that Tito guy you told us about? I have an idea percolating that might just get us to tracking the cocaine after it gets picked up." Montrose took over the lead from O'Donnell and enlisted the help of Baker and Esposito.

They talked about his idea for the next couple of hours, working different angles and finally came up with a plan. Baker and Esposito had worked with some new technology that might be the answer to tracking the cocaine.

"Let's break for today and bring in Tito tomorrow morning and convince him it's in his best interest to help us with this," O'Donnell said. "I need a decent cup of coffee."

Gabe took the agents to a small guest house on the outskirts of Arcadia. Baker and Esposito had to share a room—while Montrose and O'Donnell each had their own.

Gabe went back and picked them up after breakfast and drove them to the station to start putting a plan together. They gathered in the conference room and brought Tito in.

"Have a seat, Tito," Gabe said when Tito was escorted into the small conference/ lunch room.

"What's this all about? I told you I'm not wearing a wire, and you can't make me. I plan on staying alive for a while yet." Tito paced the small room, sounding more like a petulant child than a grown man.

"You don't have to wear a wire. You don't have to do anything except make a phone call. Call that guy you talked about, Santos." Gabe tried to reassure him.

"Why in heaven's name would I want to call a nut case like that and tell him what exactly?" He caved-in a tiny bit and sat down at the table. His legs were shaking nervously. "That guy has no soul. He shot Richie in cold blood. I don't want to be next."

"Tito, my name is Agent Gina O'Donnell. I'm with the DEA in Washington D.C." She stood up and showed him her badge. "These other men are Agents Montrose, Baker and Esposito. We have a plan that will not put you in any danger."

"Just listen, okay?" Gabe asked, putting a hand on Tito's shoulder. Tito shrugged, "Whatever. I'll listen but you can't make me do anything against my will."

"You're right, so just listen," O'Donnell continued. "I'm going to let agent Montrose tell you about our plan and how you can help. If you help with this, it will go a long way with the DA when you come to trial."

"Trial? I only helped load up some packages. I didn't even know what was in them at the time."

"Tito, you aided with the receiving and distribution of illegal narcotics. You were there when Mr. Jessup was killed. That's an accessory to murder. You fled to avoid arrest."

Gabe felt sorry for the man. "You're going to trial, man. This is serious."

"Oh shit. This is so fucked up. What do you want me to do?"

Agent Montrose stood up and came over to face Tito. He held a small device in his hands. "This is a tracking device. The government has been working on it for some time now. We put it in Santos's van or in the shipment, and a satellite will tell us where it goes. You don't even have to be with it. We just need you to place it where we can get the signal."

"And how am I supposed to do that from here? They know I got arrested," Tito challenged.

"I thought about that. When you make the call, you tell them you got out on bail. Mr. Hollister felt sorry for you and put it up for you." Gabe had cleared it with Gramps to go along with the idea. "You tell Santos you need some money fast to get out of town and can help with the next delivery."

Montrose picked it up from there. "He'll pick you up and take you with him for the drop. At some point, you take this," he held out his hand to show him, "and place it either in the van or better yet in one of the packages while you are loading it."

"What if he don't want me to help with the drop? What if he tells me to get lost?"

"Then we'll have to come up with something else."

"What about the DA if Santos says no way. What about me?"

"You make the phone call; you have the deal," Gabe assured him. "The more you help, the better the deal."

"Okay, get me a phone," Tito said shaking his head. He sure as hell didn't want to make this call, but what choice did he have.

"Too bad we didn't have time to get a court order for a wiretap," Dan said.

"Around here that could take weeks," Gabe replied.

They waited patiently while Tito talked with Santos. At first, it didn't sound like it was going to work, but when he hung up the phone, Tito said, "The drop is all set for tomorrow night. He'll pick me up and take me to where the drugs will be dropped. He wouldn't tell me where it was. He didn't believe me, at first, so this had better go down right, or I'm a dead man."

Chapter Sixteen

Gabe and Dan were busy tracking down drug dealers. Gramps was teaching Hector the ropes with the cattle. Soon the trees would have to be inspected for disease, pruned and sprayed, ready for the next crop. Summer was around the corner. It was always a slow time in the groves, and Nora was bored.

Putting down the book she was reading, she stroked the cat, lying comfortably in her lap. It was getting late, and she should get to bed. Maybe she could do some deep cleaning around the house tomorrow. Stuff she never got a chance to do during the time the crop was coming in. Yuck, she didn't want to do that either.

A ride on Jasper sounded better. She could ride out on the back road for a couple of miles, pack a little lunch and stop by the Myakka River. That settled, she turned off her reading lamp, pushed Hobo to the floor and stood looking out over the grove.

A noise in the distance caught her attention. It was the same plane, the one with the misfire in the engine. She tried to locate the direction it was coming in. Picking up the binoculars that were always on the porch for bird watching, she scanned the night sky for the plane.

Following the sound of the engine, she spotted the small plane coming from the south. It came in right over the house, shaking the windowpanes. Swooping low over the packing plant, she could easily make out the identification number on the tail section. She wrote it down quickly, N6109N.

"Gotcha," she exclaimed softly, not wanting to wake Gramps. "Now where did you come from, and where are you going?" she asked herself. Putting her lamp back on, she dragged out an old county map. "You have to land somewhere."

Scanning the map, she remembered the old airport to the south east of Arcadia. It was a small field used by some of the local farmers that didn't have their own private fields to land on. It was always busy with supplies on their way in or out of there. If she remembered right, there was also a flight school there. It was publicly owned. A private airport would not work if you were trying not to be noticed.

It was too late to call Gabe. She could check out the airport and call him if she found something. No need to bother him if it was a dead end and she didn't find the plane. That settled her plan for tomorrow.

In a rancher's field, not far from where Nora stood watching, the sound of the plane's engine cut through the night silence. Gabe smiled as he thought of Nora. He could pick out the skip in the engine as it approached.

The field was lit by a full moon. Gabe and his men watched from a distance. Tito and the black van were parked on the edge of the field waiting for the plane to drop the cocaine. Dan spoke quietly with the other agents, while Gabe paced in the shadow of the trees.

The van flashed its headlights. The plane banked left and swooped down low over the field—touching down for only a minute as packages of drugs were hastily tossed out the door. The engine roared as the plane rose and skimmed the trees, rising higher in the sky and heading east.

The agents and police looked on as Tito and Santos gathered the packages and quickly placed them in the back of the van. Gabe could only hope that Tito had been able to place the tracking device in one of the packages.

The plan was to follow the van at a safe distance. The tracker was in case they lost it on the dark rural roads. Loading the agents and officers, the small caravan made its way to the main road and headed in the direction the van had taken, east towards Arcadia.

Dan kept his eyes on the direction finder, listening to the pings it made. "It's working. They're a mile or so ahead of us."

Baker and Esposito oversaw the technology used in following the signal the tracker sent out.
They followed State Road 70 East to where it turned into West Oak Street out past the Oak Street Cemetery. The van turned off a side road ahead. The tracker pinged along and then suddenly stopped moving.

"The van's stopped," Agent O'Donnell said.

"That's strange. There's not much out there," Gabe said. "Not until you come to the small airport. How could I have been so stupid? Of course, the airport. I found it on the map back in my office right before we left. It just didn't register. I'm still learning my way around here. It's the only public one around here. There are a couple of private ones, but strangers would be found out right away at one of those."

"Let's go on and see where the tracker stopped. Maybe they're at a house or building down that road," Agent Montrose said.

With Dan and his DEA agents in the lead, they followed the signal down a deeply rutted road. "This car was not designed for this," O'Donnell said as another bone-rattling hole rocked the vehicle.

"I can't take this down any farther. I'll break an axle or something. Last thing I need is for the drug runners to find a DEA car broken down out here," Dan said.

Stopping, he got out and walked back to Gabe's car. "My car won't make it on this road. It's too low. At least we have a good idea where they're heading."

"Let's go back to my office. I'll send someone out tomorrow in a truck that can handle the road," Gabe said. He was upset with himself and disappointed that they couldn't continue the surveillance and follow the van to see where it was off-loading the drugs.

Turning the vehicles around in the dark was a struggle. One almost lost it and would have ended up in a water-filled ditch on the edge of the narrow dirt road. Riding back in silence, they were all thinking the same thing. The Arcadia Airport was the key. Tomorrow, they would put something together to catch whoever was the head of this operation.

A couple of questions roamed in Gabe's mind. How would they know which plane had carried the drugs? Why drop the drugs in the orange groves? Seemed he had more questions than answers.

The smell of coffee woke Nora in the morning. She had tossed and turned most of the night. "Hi Gramps," Nora said, drowsily stifling a yawn.

"Well, you look like you had a bad night," the old man said, pouring coffee for himself and Nora.

"I had a lot on my mind. I saw that plane again last night. Maybe Gabe and Dan saw it, too," she said.

"I sure would like to get this drug business over with. I can't figure why people have to get mixed up with that stuff."

"It's the money, Gramps. There's a lot of money in the drugs." Nora sat at the table with her hands around the warm cup.

"You want any breakfast this morning, sweetheart?" Gramps threw some bacon in an old cast iron pan. "I can fix you up some eggs. Rosita is having a hard time with that nephew of hers. She will be here a bit late today."

"No on the eggs, but thanks. I've got a couple of errands to run this morning. I should be back in time for lunch. Are you working with Hector this morning?" She hoped to distract him about where exactly she was going.

"I thought we would go look at the bull you found over in Sarasota. I'll call the guy after I eat and clean up here. I hope it's still for sale." Gramps tipped his eggs onto a couple of pieces of buttered toast on his plate. He sat down and started to cut into his breakfast. "We haven't heard from your two suitors lately. I'm wondering how they're doing?"

"Gramps, they are not my suitors!" Nora exclaimed as Rosita came in the kitchen door.

"Suitors, Madre Dios, finally my little dove has suitors?" Rosita questioned from the kitchen doorway. She came in and grabbed a kitchen towel.

"I don't have suitors. I have male friends," Nora said a little too strongly and stormed out of the room calling back, "Quit trying to marry me off."

"I've got my money on Gabe," Gramps laughed.

"I think so, too," Rosita said with a smile as she helped to clear up the breakfast things. "Mr. Frank, my nephew is visiting from Columbia. He is the son of my sister. He is so lazy that no woman in her right mind will have him. I want him to meet you and Miss Nora sometime, but he is always too busy doing nothing."

"Not a problem, Rosita. Maybe I can make some calls and find him a bit of work while he is here," Gramps offered.

"Thank you, but I do not want him to be a bad worker and make it look bad for you," Rosita said.

"I understand. The offer is there if you need it." Gramps patted Rex on the head and proceeded to feed the old mutt his breakfast while Rosita finished cleaning up the kitchen.

Nora went upstairs to get dressed and was ready to head out. Rex had finished his breakfast, and she found him sleeping on the back seat of the jeep. Not wanting to disturb him, she took the battered Ford truck they used around the grove and headed out to Arcadia.

Chapter Seventeen

"How did that van disappear last night?" Dan asked as he paced Gabe's small office. "We were following that signal right until it turned down the road to the airport."

Sergeant Alvarez knocked on the frame of the open door. "Got a minute?" he asked.

Gabe waved him in. Alvarez put a small electronic devise on the desk in front of Gabe. Dan reached over and picked it up. "This is the tracker I gave Tito to put in one of the packages of drugs," Dan said.

"I had a couple of men go back down the road where we lost the signal. They found this about halfway down—right after a big pothole. My guess is it never made it into the van at all. I think Tito couldn't put it where we wanted it, so he put it on the bumper and it got jarred off when it hit that hole.

"Good thing they didn't find the tracker. That might have been hard for Tito to explain," Gabe said. He stood and looked at the county map pinned on the wall behind his desk. Then he turned, put his hat on his head, and checked the gun in his holster. "You game to go check out that airport? I've got a feeling that's where that plane is," he said to Dan.

"Do you want the other agents in on this?" Gabe asked.

"Not yet. Let's go talk to them. We're just going to check it out for now," Dan said.

They walked down the short hallway to the room in which the agents had set up shop. Agent O'Donnell was pacing with a stale cup of coffee. She grimaced after each sip. "When are you guys going to learn how to make a decent cup of coffee?"

"Probably when you show them how," Montrose quipped. That kind of remark really rankled O'Donnell. Women were not the only ones who could make coffee.

"You want fresh coffee; there's the pot," O'Donnell said indicating the coffee set up in the corner.

"Why, when we have you," Montrose answered.

"You're such a jerk," she retaliated.

"Ok, ok, enough, we have more important issues than who makes the coffee," Dan said—walking to a board that had pictures of the van, Tito, and Mr. Jessup's dead body lying on his bed, bloody and beaten. "Gabe and I are going to take a ride and check out a little public access airport south east of Arcadia. That's the general direction the van was heading when we had to turn back.

"The tracking device was found and brought back. So, we know we're heading in the right area. There are hangers and storage areas there that the drug dealers could be using. They never came back to the machine shop. It's evident they've moved their operation.

"We've had a stake-out at the machine shop, and there has been no one coming or going anywhere near there since we found Hernandez. I think we spooked them a bit. We'll call if we find anything interesting. For now, it's just recon," Dan said, outlining their idea.

"I'm not too crazy about you two going on your own," O'Donnell said. Being a female in the DEA was hard enough. She didn't like being sidelined. Government positions for women didn't come along that often, and she wanted to prove that women were just as capable as the men in the field.

"You can come along if you want, but like I said, we're only checking out the airport to see if the plane could possibly be landing there. It might not amount to anything. There are several private airfields the plane could be using," Gabe told her.

"Outside in five—anyone that wants to go," Dan said and left the room.

"That leaves us to find a decent cup of coffee," Montrose smirked.

"How about some donuts to go with the coffee, too?" Baker asked.

"Yeah, let's check out that diner. I could use some breakfast," Esposito added.

Agent O'Donnell and Gabe followed Dan outside, leaving the others to find the diner and a decent cup of coffee.

Nora had a head start of a couple of hours before Gabe and Dan left the station. She felt her teeth would be jarred right out of her head as the old truck bounced through the potholes on the airport access road. The truck had high ground clearance, but she had to hold tight to the wheel to keep control.

About five hundred yards along, Nora saw an opening in the chain link fence. Following it around to a group of buildings and a couple of hangers, she saw a sign for the Lenox Flight School on one of the hangers. Across the runway were a couple of more buildings and a "Welcome to the Arcadia Municipal Airport" sign.

Pulling the truck behind one of the buildings, she got out and thought, "What the hell am I doing out here?" It dawned on her how foolish she was not to tell anyone where she was going. She should have called Gabe and told him about the plane and the registration number. *"Too late now,"* she thought.

She wandered around to the front and noticed some rundown buildings and houses across the street from the end of the runway. Someone yelled at her to get out of the way as a small plane landed on the runway.

"What do you think you're doing, lady? You almost got run over. We might be out in the sticks, but it's still an active runway." A man in a four-wheeler turned and chased the plane to where it stopped in front of one of the hangers.

Nora hadn't realized that her wandering had brought her smack dab in the middle of the plane's path. She walked up to the man and apologized, "I'm so sorry. This is my first time here. I used to fly and thought I might take it up again," she said. "Is the airport open all the time . . . at night, too?" She was hoping to find some answers that might lead to the plane she had seen.

"We close the terminal at night, but a few planes do land after dark. They have to call ahead and file their flight plan and ETA so we're ready for them. We have to light the runway and such. No plane lands after dark that we don't know about. Planes don't land here without runway lights, it's too dangerous. There is always someone here day and night checking the planes in and out."

"Oh, I don't think I'd like to land at night. Do many planes do that?" she asked.

"Look lady, I have another plane to make ready for the next student. Check in the office and my girl, Shana, can answer your questions or sign you up for a lesson." The man put the four-wheeler in gear and went to check out the small Piper Cub for the next lesson.

Nora followed the sign and found the flight school in one of the row of houses and buildings she had spotted across the road. A bell over the door tinkled as she walked in. A young girl about twenty came out of a back room. The girl had a lot more makeup on than was called for during the day, and large gold hoop earrings dangled from her ears.   "Hi there, what can I do for you today? Interested in some flying lessons?"

"Maybe, if your name is Shana," Nora answered. "I was talking to a man outside, and he sent me to you. I hope you can help me. I'm looking for a particular plane. I've seen it flying around, and I like the looks of it and wanted to find out if it's been landing here. I have the registration numbers from the tail."

"Why that plane?" Shana asked. She looked back over her shoulder and back to Nora.

"Like I said, I like the looks of it. I used to fly and thought I might take it up again. If I do, I'll need a plane. We have an orange grove near here, and it might be a good idea to be able to fly up to Tampa or Jacksonville to talk to distributors." Nora was thinking it up as she went along.

Shana seemed to relax and accept Nora's story. "We keep a log of the planes that fly in and out of here. What's the registration?" she asked, flipping open a large ledger book on the desk.

"The number is N6109N," Nora replied.

Shana scanned the book, flipping a few pages, "Here it is. That plane is a Piper Malibu."

"I like the sound of that. Do you have information on who owns it? I'd love to see inside and see what the controls are like and how many passengers I could fit in there. You know, like for a girls' weekend away. I'm sure my friends would love that." Nora was enjoying herself but nervous at the same time. She wondered just how much more information she could pry out of the girl.

"It says the plane is out of Miami, a company called M&C Enterprises. They land at night and take off in the morning, so your chances of getting a look inside are pretty low."

"Oh, well," Nora said. "It was worth a try. Do you have a list of your prices for lessons? I'm sure I'd only need a couple to have me flying again."

Shana handed her a pamphlet and said, "Is there anything else I can do for you?"

"No thanks, you've been very helpful, and I'll call for some lessons soon."

Nora walked out the door. The bell tinkled again.

Shana stood watching her walk back across the street. A tall, dark man came up behind her and nuzzled her neck. "What did she want?" he asked.

Shana told him that Nora was interested in his plane and some flying lessons. "She likes your plane. You should be happy."

His dark eyes followed Nora. "I think I'll find out if she needs more information," he said.

"Santos, where are you going? She's just looking for a plane to buy."

"Maybe, but I'm going to make sure," he said fingering the knife at his waist.
Santos followed Nora from the office. He saw her looking in the hangers, checking registration numbers. "Ola Chica," he called pleasantly as he approached her.

Nora jumped. "You startled me."

"Shana said you were looking for a plane, a Piper Malibu?"

"Yes, I've seen one around and thought I might like one," Nora answered.

"You live around here?"

"Not far," Nora was starting to be afraid.

"Pretty lady like you all alone out here?" His smile was like a snake, his gold tooth catching the morning sun. "Snooping in business that doesn't concern you? You're Nora Hollister. You live right next door to that Jessup place."

Nora was scared. He knew her, but how? "Yes, that's how I saw the plane. My parent used to fly, and I did too for a bit."

"I'll show you one. It's in the next hanger. You can have a close-up look." Santos gave her a hard shove, which almost knocked her to the ground and steered her in the direction of the hanger.

Nora felt the muzzle of a gun pushed in her back, urging her to move faster.

He reached around her and opened the small door beside the closed sliding entry doors for the planes.

She tried to protest but got a shove that sent her tumbling through the door and onto the concrete floor. "Why are you doing this? How do you know me?" Nora asked, sitting on the floor trying not to cry. She didn't want to give him the satisfaction.

How would anyone know where she was? She hadn't told anyone what she was up to. No one was going to come to her rescue. Only now did she realize how stupid that had been.

She heard a muffled moan from behind her. Looking around, she saw Tito, bloody and bruised, tied to a chair with silver duct tape over his mouth. "What have you done to him?"

The plane was there in the hanger, N6109N— the plane she had seen dropping the drugs. She was in deep trouble.

"Same as what's going to happen to you. You think you're so clever—coming around, asking questions." Santos grabbed her by the arm and jerked her up to stand on her feet. Grabbing another chair, he tossed her into it beside Tito.

"I still don't know who you are," Nora said. "You can let us go. Get in the plane and fly away."

"No, that doesn't work for me. I need you to tell me who you told you were coming here?" he answered, tying her hands behind the chair.

"No one knows. I didn't tell anyone."

"I wish I could believe you. No one will miss Tito. But you . . . you are a big problem. Tito told me about working with the DEA. Of course, I had to loosen his tongue a bit. He told me about the D.C. agents and putting the tracker on my van."

Santo suddenly turned his attention to Tito and hit him with his fist in the jaw. Tito's head snapped back and forward resting on his chest. He was unconscious.

"Tell me who you are if you're going to kill me. I deserve to know the name of my murderer," she said with more courage than she felt.

He strolled around rubbing his chin thinking, "I guess it can't hurt now. My aunt, Rosita, works for you and your grandfather. Since I was going to be around for a while, I needed someplace to live. She and that husband of hers have been after me to get a job. That's funny because I have a job. The Medellin Cartel pays me more than they will ever make.

"Pablo Escobar came to me himself when I was a boy playing soccer on the dirty streets of Columbia. At first, I was just a runner for the drugs. I worked hard and moved up the ladder. He trusts me with the operation here, and he pays me well. I am only known to the fools that do my bidding. Now you know, and now I must make sure you can't tell anyone."

Nora was struggling, trying to free her hands, the rough rope chaffing against her wrists. All the while she was trying to keep him talking, stalling for time to figure out a way to save herself, praying that Gabe would come.*"No one knows I'm here. Why didn't I tell Gabe? Because he would have stopped you,"* she answered herself.

"Ok, since you're going to kill me anyway, I'm curious. Why drop the drugs in the orange groves when you can land here?" Nora asked.

"That old man out there is always around, snooping. He checks out the planes, the hangers. There is nowhere he doesn't stick his nose. We don't keep the drugs at the airport. We drop them and take them to a safe place away from prying eyes. The plane lands, refuels and heads back to Miami for more," he gloated.

CHAPTER EIGHTEEN

Gabe, Dan and Agent O'Donnell were jarred as they drove along the rutted road to the airport. Spotting the same entrance Nora had, they followed the road and drove to one of the hangers.

"Ok, where do we begin?" Dan asked.

"Let's take a walk around. It's not like there's a lot of places to hide a plane. Only two hangers and a couple of smaller buildings," Gabe suggested.

"There's a guy over there by that plane. Looks like he might know about what goes on around here." Gina took off in that direction—while Gabe and Dan split up and walked around the hangers.

Gabe recognized the battered-up farm truck as one he had seen at the Hollister's, parked behind the hanger. "Shit! I'll strangler her when I find her."

He walked quickly and caught up with Dan. "Nora is here somewhere. Her truck is back there."

They spotted Gina talking with a man on the runway. "So, you really don't know who is using the airport at night?"

"Look lady, I'm telling you the same as I told the other one. Check in the office. I'm only maintenance around here. I check that the planes don't fall out of the sky once they're up there. That's all I do."

Gabe and Dan heard the last of the conversation. Dan signaled Gina to come away. Out of the man's hearing, Gabe said, "Nora's here."

"Where?" Gina asked. As much as she admired Nora's spunk, she knew the danger she could be in.

"My guess is she saw that plane same as we did last night. She figured out the plane has to land somewhere and that this is the most likely place around. I told her not to get involved, but knowing her and how head strong she can be . . ."

"I get it, but if she's not with her truck, where is she? We have to find her and fast," Dan said—concern in his voice.

O'Donnell spoke up, "We need to call for more help. If she was okay, we would have seen her."

"Maybe, and maybe not," Gabe said—clearly worried. Determined to find Nora, he walked around the hangers. Behind the last hanger he heard voices. One was Nora's. The other he didn't know. He drew his gun and signaled for Gina and Dan to come over. "I hear Nora in there. Find a window, so we can see what's going on."

Keeping close to the building, Dan and Gina scouted for a window. Finding one, Dan helped to boost Gina up so she could see in. The window was filthy, but she could see enough.

Signaling to be let down, she said, "Nora is tied to a chair beside Tito. He looks in bad shape. She's holding her own and keeping him talking. There is a back door behind a plane, so we might be able to get in without being seen."

Making their way back to Gabe, they filled him in on trying for the back door.

"We'll need to distract the guy with the gun. I'll take the front door. While he's talking to me you two go in the back," Gabe said.

"You're taking a chance he won't fire first and ask questions later," Dan said.

Movement caught Gina's eye. "Look, they're going to have a distraction after all."

They watched as Shana tottered up to the hanger on high heels and a skirt up to her ass. "I'll bet she's not taking flying lessons," Dan said, raising his eyebrows at the leggy brunette.

Shana opened the door and walked in. They could hear her yell, "Santos, what in hell are you doing?"

"Just tidying up loose ends," he sneered.

"You don't have to do this, Santos," Nora said.

"I've already killed one man, so a couple more folks won't make that much of a difference.
You just couldn't stay out of this," he yelled back at the young girl. He ran his hands over his face trying to think. He had three people who knew too much.

"Get over with them." He waved his gun at her, telling her to stand beside Nora and Tito. She moved to do as she was told.

Gabe came in the front door with his gun drawn. Santos heard him and grabbed Shana—holding her in front of him like a shield, his gun at her head.

"Let her go, Santos. You're not getting out of this," Gabe said—trying to judge if Santos would really shoot the girl. He had to figure he would. He observed Gina and Dan creeping cautiously in the back door. If he could keep Santos talking, they might surprise him.

"How do you figure on getting away, Santos?" Gabe asked him.

"How about I have Chica fly me out of here?" he answered.

"I haven't flown a plane for years," Nora shouted.

"Just like riding a bike," he said. He backed up, dragging Shana with him.

Nora had managed to wiggle her hands free. As she spied an open tool box a few feet away, she side-stepped towards it—keeping an eye on Santos and Gabe. A large wrench was lying on the top of other tools in the box. She picked up it up and waited until Santos was close enough to her—whacking the wrench on his head with all her strength. He went down in a heap. Shana ran a few feet and sank to her knees sobbing.

Gabe rushed to Nora, cradling her in his arms. Gina ran to Shana, and Dan put cuffs on the unconscious Santos.

"Are you alright?" Gabe asked Nora, brushing her hair out of her eyes.

"I'm fine now," she said, looking into his eyes. She planted a firm kiss on his lips which he returned, fire burning inside.

"You sure do pack a wallop," Gabe said when he caught his breath.

Dan checked on Tito, "He'll need an ambulance, but he should be okay. I think Santos has a concussion. He'll need the hospital, too."

The maintenance man, Shana's father, came through the door. "What the hell is going on here?" he yelled, seeing his daughter crying on the floor with Agent Gina O'Donnell standing over her.

Dan called the ambulance and the agents waiting at the station, while Gabe and Nora tried to fill him in on how his daughter had gotten mixed up with a drug-dealing murderer. It didn't go over well. "What were you thinking?" he yelled at the poor girl huddled on the floor.

"I thought he loved me. He took me places and bought me things," she protested. "None of the other guys around here ever did that."

"I should have known something was up with the way your skirts kept getting shorter and the make-up got thicker. Your mom was the same way before she left with that sky jockey she took up with. Get up off that floor and come on home. We have some talking to do."

"Sir, I'm Agent Gina O'Donnell with the DEA, Drug Enforcement Agency. I'm going to have some questions for Shana here." She put out her hand, and the older man took it. "I'm Rusty Fairfield, Shana's dad and maintenance around the field. You need her for anything, let me know, and she'll be there. You have my word."

"Thanks, Mr. Fairfield, we'll be in touch." Gina watched father and daughter head over to the office across the street. They probably lived in that row of houses facing the field. They arranged for her to be taken to the station—where her dad could pick her up later. She didn't envy Shana when her dad got her home. No Sir.

"So, what have we got—the guy that drove the van, right? But who's been flying the plane, and where in heaven's name are the drugs?" Dan asked, finishing his calls and joining the others.

"Let's hope Tito pulls through and can answer some of those questions. I'll get some officers to watch the plane and see who shows up to fly it out of here," Gabe said, holding Nora close to him. "Your Gramps is going to skin you alive when he finds out what you have been up to," he said, turning her to face him. "You could have been killed. Get in your truck, and I'll follow you home."

Dan, Gina and Gabe were close behind Nora when she pulled up to her back door. Rex came down the steps barking at the unfamiliar vehicle.

Gramps opened the door, "Rex, quiet. They're friends." Rex looked up at Gramps and then back to the people getting out. He wagged his tail and wandered over to sniff and greet his visitors.

Gina bent down and gave the dog a scratch behind his ears—becoming his new best friend.

"Gramps this is Agent Gina O'Donnell with the DEA," Dan said introducing her.

"Pleased to meet you, Ma'am," Gramps said, curiosity dancing in his eyes as he looked at Nora and her guests. "What have you been up to, young lady?" he asked, addressing Nora.

"I think this needs a full pot of coffee," Gabe suggested.

"And some of your Macallan's," added Nora.

Rosita started to fill the coffee pot. "Rosita, I have something to tell you about your nephew, Mateo—'Santos,' isn't it?" Nora asked gently.

"You've met my Mateo?" Suddenly it dawned on her that this would not be good news. She sank down in one of the kitchen chairs. Nora reached over and took her.

"Santos is involved in the drug running around here. He was at Henry Jessup's that night."

"Oh, Madre Dios, I knew he was up to no good." Tears were running down her face. "How can I tell my sister this?"

"Don't worry, I'll help you." Nora wiped a tear from her eye and poured them both a healthy shot of whiskey.

CHAPTER NINETEEN

Sitting around the table, Nora told Gramps how she had spotted the plane and had gone to the airport to see if it had landed there. "It was all perfectly innocent. A quick look around, a few questions and I was going to leave," Nora said. "But then this guy Santos comes out and tells me he knows who I am and where I live. Gramps, he's Rosita's nephew."

Dan and Gabe stood to leave. "We have reports to write; we must check on Tito and Santos; and we need to have someone watch that plane to grab the pilot. The list is endless," Dan said. Gina joined them, "I need to report to the DEA in Washington. I have to send one of the agents out to talk to Shana. I might do it myself. I have a feeling she might relate better to a female."

"I'll go with you, Gina," Nora said—ready to charge out again.

"Oh, no you don't," they all answered at once.

"You are going to stay here," Gabe said.

"I'll tie her up if I have to," Gramps said.

"Ah, come on, I can talk to Tito or Shana. I can't possibly get into trouble there," Nora pleaded. "You guys have your hands full, and I can help.”

Dan hung his head and talked softly to Gabe with Nora listening. "We have a proposition. You can go and talk to Tito—only Tito. Stay away from Santos. You have to take Agent Esposito with you.

“Gina can go to see Shana and take Baker. Agent Montrose will stand guard over Santos. That should make him happy. These drug cartels are vicious and might try to silence Santos so he can't give up the man pulling the strings here.

"You're not going to let me tie her up, are you?" Gramps questioned.

"No, not this time," Gabe said. "If I leave her here, she'll take off and do God knows what. At least she'll have an agent with her, and she might be able to get something useful out of Tito."

Gramps agreed reluctantly. He knew Gabe was right. Nora would not stand for being on the sidelines now. Talking to Tito would keep her busy and safe. It was better to know where she was and that someone was with her who could protect her.

Back at the station, Dan outlined the assignments to the agents, and Montrose went ballistic. "Why do I have to babysit an unconscious guy in the hospital? I could do the interview with that guy Tito or the girl, what's her name?"

Gina knew just how to handle Montrose. "Only you have the experience to watch over a dangerous murderer. What if he wakes up and takes a nurse hostage? What if the cartel sends someone to shut him up permanently? You're the best man for the job. Baker and Esposito don't have the instincts to spot trouble that you have." She could see the wheels turning in his head, and he took the bait.

"You're right. They're too new at the job," he said—puffing up like a rooster at the praise.

"Let's get a move on and end this thing," Dan said, holstering his gun.

At that moment, the phone on Gabe's desk rang. He listened for a few seconds and put the receiver down.

"The men watching the plane caught the pilot as he was getting ready to take off. Rusty Fairchild let my men know he was there. He's not talking yet, but he will once we get him in here. I'll see if I can loosen him up for when you get back," he said and watched Nora as she headed out of the office to talk to Tito.

His gut churned, thinking of what might have happened to her. Here she was heading out again. He hoped Esposito could handle her and keep her safe. He hoped they would all be safe.

CHAPTER TWENTY

Nora and Agent Esposito arrived at the information desk of Manatee Memorial Hospital the same time as Special Agent Montrose. The volunteer at the desk was pleasant and helpful—directing them to the floors and rooms they were looking for.

They shared the elevator to the third floor where special Agent James Montrose got off to babysit Santos, who was handcuffed to the bed. Nora and Esposito went up to the fourth floor to the ward where they would find a slightly-bruised Tito.

Nora opened the door slowly. Tito was watching some game show on the TV. His face was a black and blue mess with a couple of butterfly bandages under his eye and one up by his hair line. A bad split lip had him sucking juice from a straw.

Seeing Nora with the agent standing behind her, he shut off the television and tried to pull himself up straighter in the bed. Feeling a bit used by the DEA, he asked, "What are you doing here? Haven't I suffered enough for you guys? I did what you asked, and look where it got me." He was mad, upset that he had let himself get involved with Richie Cantura and his crazy plans.

"We're sorry it worked out like this," Nora said.

"Yeah, me too. It wasn't supposed to go down like this," Agent Esposito agreed.

"There are a few questions the DEA thought you might help them with," Nora said approaching his bed. He tried to put his juice on the little table beside his bed, and Nora reached out to help him. He gave her a nod. She took the carton from him and placed it on the table.

"I've had some time to think about how this all started and why," Tito said, taking a deep breath. "It's all my fault. I was cheating the workers and deserved to be fired. I didn't have to go with Richie and get involved with Santos and the drug drops. In that hanger with Santos beating the shit out of me, I learned that I deserved every hit, every punch he gave me."

"Tito, you don't have to . . ."

Tito stopped her. "No, Nora, I do."

"I thought about how I grew up poor. I hated every minute I spent in the cigar factories of Ybor City. I wanted what the rich guys had, but I didn't want to work for it. My family gave me all they could. They gave me a life I would never have had in Cuba. We had a roof over our heads, food on the table, decent clothes to wear. They gave me the opportunities of a good education, and I threw it in their faces."

Tito started to cry. "What did I get trying to get rich my way—thrown in jail, beaten up by a crazy, sick lunatic? He would have killed me if you guys hadn't shown up to save my ass."

Nora handed him a tissue to wipe the tears running down his face.

"Thanks, Ms. Hollister. I don't deserve your kindness. Tell Gramps I'm sorry."

Esposito pulled up a chair. Nora found a perch on the bed beside Tito. Nora gave Tito's hand a squeeze, and the agent asked his questions. After a few minutes, he gave Tito and Nora some time alone and sat outside the door.

Downstairs, the volunteer receptionist gave someone else information to Mateo Santos and Tito Ramirez's rooms. In the elevator, he checked his gun and screwed the silencer onto the muzzle. He watched the numbers change above the door and got out on the fourth floor.

He had his orders and twenty-five thousand dollars in his off-shore account. He was counting on getting the other half when he finished his assignment. He was a Cartel hitman, hired to kill Mateo Santos and Tito Ramirez, a double header and a double pay day.

Down the hallway, he saw a man in a suit sitting in a chair outside the room Ramirez was in. He had to come up with a distraction. Luck had placed the doctors' lounge across from the elevator doors.

Walking in, he nodded hello to a doctor helping himself to coffee. The doctor nodded back and left with his coffee. The killer picked up a lab coat from the back of a chair, put it on, flipped the ID on the pocket so the photo didn't show and walked out. Passing the nurses' station, he picked up an unattended stethoscope and threw it around his neck.

"Hey there, how's our patient today?" he asked the man, who he assumed was a federal agent, as he pushed the door open to the room. "I'll be just a moment."

The assailant was surprised to see Nora sitting in a chair beside Tito. She got up and said, "I'll leave you with him. He's resting now. I hope you don't have to wake him up. I'll be right outside if he needs me." Compassion and concern registered in her voice.

"Do you want to get some coffee or anything?" Nora asked the agent.

Esposito didn't answer right away. He was thinking about cowboy boots. What doctor would wear worn-down cowboy boots? Alarm bells went off in his head.

"Cowboy boots?" he muttered.

"What?" Nora asked.

He signaled Nora to be quiet—putting his index finger to his lips. The agent got up and went into Tito's room. Easing open the door, he saw the gun with the silencer pointed at the sleeping figure in the bed. Tito must have sensed the danger and opened his eyes—as a shocked and bewildered expression crept across his face.

"No, you don't have to do this. I won't say a word," Tito pleaded.

"So sorry. It's nothing personal. It's my job, and I'm really good at it."

"Not so good this time. Special Agent Esposito DEA," Esposito said. "Put the gun down now."

"I don't think so, Agent." The man swung the gun towards the agent—ready to fire. Tito made a live-or-die decision and threw the tray lying on his bedside table at the man with the gun.

Startled, the man took his attention from the agent for an instant. It was all Esposito needed. He sprang towards the man, and the gun went off. Searing pain in his shoulder told him he had been hit. The assailant ran out the door, knocking Nora to the floor.

"Push that damn button and get some help in here," the agent shouted to Tito.

"Yeah, yeah, okay," Tito said scrambling to find the button to call the nurse.

One floor up, Montrose saw the hospital staff running around and whispering about a shooting. He stopped one of the nurses, "What's going on?"

"Someone tried to kill one of the patients," the nurse said before rushing off.

"Which patient?" he called after her but got no answer.

He went to the nurse's station and insisted that someone call down to get Agent Esposito on the phone.

He waited for what seemed like an eternity before he heard, "Agent Montrose, this is Doctor Gallagher. Your friend Agent Esposito is on his way to the OR right now."

Montrose interrupted him, "In the OR? What happened? How bad is he hurt?"

"He's fine. He took a bullet to the shoulder, but it missed the brachial artery by a fraction. The young lady with him was knocked to the ground but only her dignity was hurt," the doctor explained.

"What about Tito Ramirez? Was he shot?"

"Mr. Ramirez wasn't hurt and can go home in the morning. His head injury did cause a slight concussion, but he will recover just fine as well."

"When can I talk to Agent Esposito?" Montrose asked, calmer now that he had some information.

"He'll be in recovery for a couple of hours after surgery. You can see him after that. We'll keep him overnight. You can take everyone home tomorrow morning. I have hospital security sitting outside Mr. Ramirez's room for now."

"Thanks, Doc. I appreciate you taking the time to talk to me."

Nora appeared at his side as he was hanging up the phone. I came down to tell you, but I see you already know what's happened."

"Are you okay?" he asked.

"Yeah, just shaken up," Nora said, leaning on the nurse's station. "Do you think the hit man will come after Santos?"

"I don't know. But you're right about it being a hit. I'll call Dan and have him and Gabe come here. It's a little late to lock down the hospital, but I'll have security check everyone leaving the hospital. I'll have someone check the security cameras too.

He picked up the phone again and had the operator connect him with security. Then, he called the police station and filled Gabe in. Gabe and Dan were on their way before he hung up the phone.

Cesar Montoya stood in the supply closet looking out the small window at the nurses and doctors running around. Security men were walking up and down the hall. He checked his gun again. He was watching Mateo Santos's room. He still had a job to do. He had been paid, and he always finished the contract, no matter how difficult it was.

The girl he had knocked over upstairs was talking to someone at the nurse's station. They had their backs to him. Now was his chance. He might not get another one. He grabbed a couple of small items off the shelf and casually walked out of the closet and across the hall to Santos's room.

Nora turned and saw a doctor enter Santos's room. Strange, she thought. The doctor had cowboy boots on. "Hadn't Esposito said something about cowboy boots?"

She gave Montrose a poke with her elbow and nodded with her head towards the room across the hall.

"The hit man's in Santos's room. I saw him," Nora whispered. She didn't want to alarm anyone or cause any noise that might alert the assailant.

Montrose drew his gun and crossed to listen at the door.

"I have a message for you from Escobar. He don't like loose ends," Cesar said.

"I'm not a loose end. I haven't said anything to anyone," Santos stated. All his bravado disappeared at the sight of a gun pointed his way.

"And you won't either," Cesar raised his gun. Santos tried to back away as far as the bed would let him. He was cuffed to the side rail, but panic drove him to try and break free.

Montrose charged in the door just as Cesar pulled the trigger. The gun went off, the bullet lodging in the ceiling. Both men went down in a heap. Cesar was up first and kicked the agent hard in the ribs, knocking the wind out of him.

Nora was about to rush in as Cesar opened the door. She froze on the spot. He stopped for an instant and took off down the hall. Nora grabbed a bed pan off a passing cart and threw it at him as hard as she could. It caught him high in the back, throwing him off balance, and he fell. Without thinking she ran up, picked up the bedpan again and slammed it into his head—knocking him out. She sat down beside Montoya, catching her breath, not quite believing what she had just done.

Gabe pulled her up off the floor and encircled her in a tight embrace. He and Dan had arrived a split second before in time to watch her clobber Cesar Montoya with the bedpan. Some of the nurses were standing around clapping at her heroics.

Dan walked over and took Cesar's hands and threw a pair of cuffs on him. Gabe watched Montrose stumbled out of Santos's room holding his bruised ribs. When he saw Cesar on the floor, he assumed that Dan or Gabe had apprehended him.

"Well done, Dan," Montrose said clapping Dan on the shoulder.

"I had nothing to do with it. Nora's pretty deadly with a bedpan," Dan said looking at Gabe holding Nora. She was shaking with her head buried in Gabe's shoulder.

"What? Nora?" Montrose said trying to understand what had happened. "She's a civilian and a girl to boot."

"I'll tell you all about it later. We have to get this guy in jail and see what O'Donnell and Baker have learned from Shana. I want to see if what Tito said lines up with her story.

Agents O'Donnell and Baker were at the station when they all returned. Cesar Montoya was now also cuffed to a bed in Manatee Memorial Hospital.

Gina was stunned when she learned how Nora had taken down Montoya. She hugged Nora around the shoulders. "Well, seems we girls can pack a punch when we have to, huh?"

Nora was a bit embarrassed by the attention. "I didn't even think. It all happened so fast. I couldn't let him get away."

"Let's hear what you got from Shana Fairchild," Dan said.

Gina took a seat at the table and opened her note pad. "Santos took advantage of Shana so he could get information about the airfield and surrounding area. She understands that now. He never told her about the drug business. She thought he was a business man and loved her. The poor girl hoped he would take her with him when he left. Santos lied to her every step of the way." Gina got up to pour herself some water from the cooler in the corner. She paced a bit as she talked.

"She overheard him talking to someone once about moving the operation closer to the field."

"That must be when we found that tool shop and Manny what's-his-name," Gabe said.

"Sounds about right," Dan agreed.

"Shana didn't understand what he was talking about but that it seemed urgent. A few days later he showed up with Ramirez and was troubled about something. She knew that they were keeping something in a building nearby, but she didn't know where."

"Okay, so they moved the drug operation closer to the airfield. I bet he got spooked when Jessup turned up dead. We have to get Tito to tell us where the drugs are being kept. The cartel will want to find them before we do," Dan said. He was drawing a time line on the white board at the front of the room, filling in the blanks.

"Tomorrow, we collect Ramirez, Santos, and Montoya from the hospital. We'll split them up and see who wants to talk first," Dan continued.

"Don't forget Agent Esposito," Nora said. It was late in the afternoon by now, and she knew Gramps would start to worry. "Look, guys, this is all fascinating, but I've got to get home. Gramps will be worried, and I have to feed Jasper."

"Who's Jasper?" Gina asked.

"Jasper is her horse," Gabe said rolling his eyes and smiling. "Come on Nora, I'll take you home. You've had enough excitement for one day."

When they pulled up to Nora's house, Rex went wild barking and dancing around Gabe's vehicle. Gramps came out to see what had set off the dog. "Quiet—you foolish thing. You know Nora and Gabe," he shouted at the dog. "'Bout time you got home. I was ready to send out the National Guard to find you. Come on in and tell me what took you all so long."

Sitting at the kitchen table with hot coffee in their hands, Nora told Gramps about the hit man, Cesar Montoya, and his attempts to kill Tito and Mateo Santos. She conveniently left out the part about how she had hit him with the bedpan.

"Agent Montrose will be released with Tito and Santos in the morning," she told him.

"So how did this Montoya fella get caught?" Gramps asked—a bit confused on that part.

"He tripped and hit his head, knocked himself out," Nora said hastily.

"Umm, I think there is more you're not telling me, but I'll let it go for now," Gramps said reaching across the table to take Nora's hand in his big work-worn fingers. "I'm glad it all worked out, and you're safe at home," he said looking at his dear, brave granddaughter. He couldn't imagine life without her.

"I'd better go. I'm going to head home and get an early start in the morning," Gabe said. "Walk me out?" he asked Nora.

Standing beside his patrol car, Gabe took Nora's hands and drew her towards him. "What am I going to do with you? You could have been seriously hurt or killed by that maniac Santos or the Cartel's hired gun, Montoya.

"Gabe, I'm not a delicate flower that needs to be taken care of and sheltered," Nora told him.

"Oh, believe me I know that. But I want to take care of you and protect you. Nora, I think I'm falling in love with you." He held his breath waiting for her to answer.

"I feel the same way about you. Only I fell in love with you the minute you walked in the packing house to arrest Tito. I appreciate you wanting to protect me, but I won't be set aside because I'm a girl. I can ride and shoot as good as any man—better than some. I've worked in the grove and roped and branded the cattle. If you're looking for a little princess who's afraid to break a nail, then keep looking 'cause that's not me." When she finished, she looked at the ground—afraid to look at his face.

Gabe tipped her chin to look in her eyes. "You are exactly what I want, you and your Jasper, rifle, and bedpan." He took her mouth with his and possessed her, leaving no doubt in her mind what his intentions were. Her insides turned to jelly, and she wanted so much more. He released her and pushed her back to arm's length. "I think I need to talk to Gramps as soon as this drug business is over," he said.

"Yeah, you do," she replied, glassy-eyed and breathless.

"I'd better go," he said. This time he kissed her gently and walked around to the driver's door. She watched as he drove away, bringing her finger tips to her lips. Could this be real, she wondered, and her heart answered . . . yes.

CHAPTER TWENTY-ONE

"Well, you're looking mighty pleased with yourself this morning," Dan said as Gabe walked into the conference room.

"If you must know, Nora and I came to an unofficial agreement after I dropped her off at home."

"Unofficial huh, then I still have a chance?" Dan laughed.

"Not if you value your life," Gabe joked back.

"Okay, enough fooling around, Agent Baker went with Dan and brought their prisoners back this morning early," Agent Gina O'Donnell said. "Esposito will be in the hospital for a couple of more days."

Baker and Dan were sitting at the table, notebooks open and waiting. "James, what did you find out from Tito? Was he able to tell you where the drug house is?" She took her seat at the table. Gabe noticed she had a paper coffee cup from the 'By the Slice Diner' down the street. Smart girl, he thought, as he suffered with the station coffee.

Montrose flipped a couple of pages in his note book, "Yeah, he said it was on the street behind the flying school office and down a couple. It's a faded blue house with white shutters. There are usually a couple of guards there now. Apparently, Santos wasn't taking any chances after we found the tool shop." He popped a pain pill for his bruised ribs.

"I'll get a couple of officers in plain clothes to locate the house and sit on it while we decide how to finish taking this down," Gabe said. He walked down to the front desk and asked Sergeant Alvarez to arrange surveillance at the Arcadia drug house.

"Hey, you planning a party and didn't invite me?" Agent Esposito said from the doorway. His arm was in a sling to protect his shoulder.

"What are you doing out of the hospital?" Agent O'Donnell asked—looking him in the eye with motherly concern.

"I didn't want to miss the finale," Esposito pleaded.

"Okay, but stay down and out of trouble," O'Donnell told him. Questioning of Tito Ramirez and Mateo Santos took the rest of the day. Tito told them everything he knew in exchange for Witness Protection. The District Attorney's Office would handle the details after Tito testified before the Grand Jury regarding Santos. Everyone agreed that putting him in prison would be a death sentence. The Cartel had a very long reach.

Santos was not cooperating. He refused to answer any questions and had "lawyered" up. He made his one phone call and was pacing a cell waiting for a lawyer to show up. He knew the Cartel had a couple of options for handling him. They could send him a lawyer to try and get him off. Even if he was sent to prison, they could arrange to have him killed. If, by some miracle, he didn't get convicted, they could still consider him a liability and have him killed.

Who was he kidding? No matter what angle he looked at, he ended up dead. Maybe he could make a deal and ask for solitary confinement in prison. Sitting on his bunk, he tried to figure out his best option. If he left it to the Cartel, he would end up in a coffin six-feet-under.

He made up his mind. Wrapping his hand around the bars of his cell, he called out, "Guard, guard, get me Sheriff McAllister. Now."

After listening to Santos and his decision to make a deal, Gabe called the District Attorney's Office again. Melvin Atwater's secretary informed Gabe that the DA was on a call and would get back to him shortly.

Sergeant Alvarez knocked on the door to Gabe's office. A distinguished gentleman behind Alvarez pushed his way past and introduced himself. "Sheriff, my name is Tomas Moreno. I am the counsel for Mateo Santos. I shall represent him with the charges at hand." He extended his hand to greet the Sheriff. Gabe reluctantly took it.

"Mr. Moreno, Santos has decided to talk to the DA about his case. I fear you have wasted your time." Gabe felt he had just shaken hands with a reptile.

Moreno answered in heavily accented, though perfect English. "My employer might see things differently." His suit was expensive. The gold rings on his fingers and the polished shoes led Gabe to believe that the Medellin Cartel had hired him. The Cartel did not want law enforcement to have any information that might be running around in Santos's head.

"I insist on having a word alone with my client," the lawyer demanded.

"I'll arrange that for you," Gabe said, leaving the room and indicating for Alvarez to come with him. "I don't like this, but we have to follow the rules. Have Santos brought to one of the interrogation rooms."

Santos was surprised to see Moreno sitting at the table when he was brought in. His hands were left cuffed as he took a seat opposite the well-dressed man.

"Mr. Santos, my employer and yours has retained me as your counsel. It is his hope that all this can be swept under the rug, shall we say. There will be a trial, and you will be proven innocent and be a free man once again."

"I don't believe that. Tito Ramirez will testify, and I will be sent to prison. There is also Nora Hollister. I kidnapped her, and she saw what I did to Ramirez. That alone will get me jail time."

"Have no fear. There will be no one to testify against you. It will all be taken care of." Moreno smiled, and Santos thought he looked like the devil himself as a shiver went down his spine.

"I will have to think about it," Santos said. Knowing his choices were limited, he called for the guard to take him back to his cell. He was suddenly freezing—goose bumps covered his arms. He knew exactly what the lawyer meant. Tito and Nora Hollister were going to die. He had just met someone more ruthless than he, and it scared him. The Medellin Cartel had very long arms indeed.

Sitting at his desk, Gabe had a lot on his mind. "Melvin Atwater on the line, Sheriff," Alvarez called to him.

"Glad you could call me back, Mel," Gabe said. "We have a situation down here and need your help." Gabe proceeded to outline what he had proposed to Tito Ramirez and what he and Santos had discussed.

"Let's get Ramirez moved to Corrections in Hillsborough as soon as possible. We can keep him in isolation until the Grand Jury convenes. I'll set it up." Mel paused before he continued with a warning, "Gabe, anyone who might testify against Santos is in danger. The Cartel will not allow him to make a deal or go to jail. He knows too much."

"I agree. Call when you're ready to move Ramirez," Gabe said. He hung up the phone and thought of Nora. She would be in danger, too. He picked up the phone to call her when Alvarez appeared at his door again.

"Sheriff, there is movement at the drug house. It looks like they are getting ready to move the drugs out of there."

"Tell O'Donnell and her bunch to be ready to roll," he called.

By the time Gabe reached his car, the agents were out and loading up. The afternoon traffic was light for a change, and they arrived on the back road near the house in record time. Parking down where they could watch and not attract attention, they saw two black vans being loaded up with boxes. Armed guards stood watching.

"How do you want to do this?" Gabe asked Dan and Gina.

"Montrose, how are your acting skills?" Dan asked. Montrose was looking a bit scruffy. He hadn't shaved, and his clothes were rumpled.

"Why, in heaven's name, do you want to know that?" the agent asked—his eyes questioning.

"Because you are going to be a drunk and distract the guards," Dan said.

Montrose didn't like the plan, "Why me?" he asked.

"Esposito can't. He's been shot. I'm a woman; Baker is too young; and you're almost scruffy enough to pull it off," Gina said.

"I guess I win by default," Montrose shrugged—stripping off his suit jacket and tie. He loosened his shirt from his pants and with the help of O'Donnell and the others got downright dirty and disgusting. A convenient mud puddle helped to mess up his hair. A discarded beer bottle completed the masquerade.

The officers watched as Montrose wandered down the unpaved road towards the blue house where the drugs were being loaded into the vans under the watchful eyes of the guards.

"He's doing it," Esposito elbowed Gina. Montrose's acting was convincing. He had the guards coming down towards him.

"Get out of here ol' man," one of them called.

Tipping the empty bottle to his mouth, Montrose shouted, "Another beer. I have to find another beer. You got some beer? Give a guy a drink." As he got closer to the guards, he pretended to stumble and grabbed the shirt of one of them to keep from falling. "Wow! Guns," he slurred. "Are you going hunting?" He laughed like it was a big joke. "What are you hunting? Is it hunting season?"

Dan and Gina signaled for Gabe and Baker to go around and come in from the back. Esposito was to stay put and watch for trouble. With his arm in a sling, he couldn't do much. His shoulder was aching, and the pain pills had stopped working. He had failed to tell Agent O'Donnell that he had left the hospital AMA, against medical advice.

Using what cover they could find, Dan and Gina managed to close the distance to the guards. Gabe crouched and ran to the far side of one of the vans. Keeping the guards in sight, Baker followed and slid up to kneel beside the front door of the house, gun drawn and ready. He could hear voices inside.

Gina held up her hand and with the guard's attention on Montrose, she counted down, three, two, one, "Go"—then signaled the agents and Gabe to take them down.

Montrose took one of the guards by surprise and ripped the gun from his hands. Using the butt of the gun, he rammed it into the man's jaw and sent him crashing to the ground. Gabe had his gun to the other guard's back and quickly disarmed him. Dan and Gina rushed to put cuffs on them both. That done, Gabe joined Baker and stormed into the house, "Hands up! Don't move!" they both shouted to the men packing up the cocaine.

Three men were led out of the house in cuffs. "I think we did it," Gina said breathless, leaning over with her hands on her knees. In the excitement, she had forgotten to breathe. Her heart was pounding. Montrose was grinning and clapping Gabe and Dan on the back.

Esposito stood up and using his good arm, pumped his fist in the air and shouted "Yeah!"

"Let's head back to the station. Gabe, let them know we're coming," Gina said.

The small police station was not built to deal with so many prisoners. Gabe called the DA's office; Dan called the DEA in Washington. Arrangements were made to move the prisoners to Hillsborough Correctional while charges were filed.

Gabe called Nora to tell her they had the dealers in custody. "Can I come over?"

"Of course. Are you hungry? I could fix something," she offered. "We haven't eaten yet, and Rosita is visiting a cousin in Myakka. Maybe I should try and call her and see how she's handling all this?"

"Good idea. A friendly voice might be what she needs right now," Gabe said. Until that moment, Gabe didn't realize he hadn't eaten all day. "I'd like something to eat, but don't go to any trouble."

"No trouble, I'll have something ready when you arrive," she beamed. She hung up the phone and did a little twirl in the middle of the kitchen.

"I guess that was Gabe on the phone?" Gramps asked from the doorway.

Nora blushed. "Yes, they got the drug dealers and the drugs. It's over Gramps. It's over."
Skipping across the kitchen she gave the old man a hug.

"Careful tiger, old bones here," he laughed.

She sat heavily in a chair and breathed a sigh of relief. "Gabe is coming over, and I need to make him something to eat," she said, jumping up and rummaging in the fridge.

CHAPTER TWENTY-TWO

Gabe knocked on the kitchen door as Nora finished setting the table. She had made up some potato salad on a pretty platter and surrounded it with deviled eggs. Sliced ham and dill pickles along with a pitcher of cold iced tea rounded out the meal.

"Hmm, looks good," Gabe said, walking in the door.

"I hope you don't mind a cold supper," Nora answered.

"I'm not talking about supper," he said, reaching out to take her in his arms. He explored her mouth with his, running his hands up and down her back, loving the feel of her in his arms.

From the doorway, Gramps cleared his throat, "Don't mind me," he chuckled. Gramps was over the moon that Nora and Gabe had found one another. "Let's eat. You can fill us in on all the dirty details," he added as he pulled out his chair and poured tea in his glass.

Gabe helped himself and between mouthfuls of ham and potato salad filled them in on the arrest of the dealers and all the drugs they had impounded.

"It couldn't have gone down any better. No one got hurt. Except the guy Montrose cracked in the jaw," Gabe said.

"I do have to tell you that it might be awhile before Santos gets to trial. Since you will be a witness, I'm worried that the Cartel might try to stop you from testifying. I'll have a talk with the DA about getting you some protection."

"I'm a big girl. I can take care of myself," Nora protested. "After all, I have Rex as my guard dog," she laughed, looking over at Rex asleep on his back—four legs in the air.

"Some guard dog he is," Gabe said.

"Look, Nora, if you need protection, you need protection," Gramps said.

"I know, but let's see what the DA says, right, Gabe? Maybe this will be over quickly."

After supper, Gabe helped Nora clean up. "I'd love to stay, but I'm beat. I'll call you tomorrow after I talk to the DA. It all depends on the Grand Jury."

Nora and Gabe walked out to his patrol car. One kiss turned into more. Reluctantly, Gabe pulled away, "I have to go. Nora, I love you."

"I love you, too," she confessed.

He did a drum roll on the top of the car with his hands, jumped in his car, started the engine and drove away before he changed his mind and decided to stay longer. He was shocked to realize that Nora was the woman he was looking for. He had never said "I love you" to another woman. This one was special, and he was determined to hold on to her forever.

She stood in the drive, watching until his car disappeared from sight.

Gabe was in his office starting to sort through the stacks of paperwork he had. He looked up and saw Dan. "Hi there," Dan said—leaning against the entry to Gabe's office. "I guess we'll be leaving and going back to D.C. There are a lot more bad guys out there to catch."

Gabe leaned back in his chair. "It was nice having you around for a while."

"It was good working together again. Maybe I can get transferred to the Miami Office."

"It's warmer down there, and you don't speak Spanish." Gabe joked.

"Rats. Guess I'll stay in D.C."

The phone on Gabe's desk rang, interrupting their talk. "What? When?" Gabe asked. Covering the mouth piece, he told Dan, "There's been a shooting."

"Where?" Dan asked.

Gabe listened for a few more minutes. "Let me know how our men are doing. Call me back when you know more."

Dan was leaning forward in his chair, waiting to wrap his head around the latest information.

"Santos was being moved to the Hillsborough Correctional Facility this morning. They were ambushed on route 60 just outside Bartow. Two of our officers were wounded, and Santos was killed. One of the shooters was also killed. The other one was able to drive away."

"It was a Cartel hit," Dan said. "Santos had information they couldn't risk getting out. I'm guessing he had names and places that would have made business very difficult if the DEA had that information."

Gabe got up and looked at the county map behind his desk. "I have a feeling that this drug thing is going to get a whole lot worse in the coming years."

"The last couple of presidents—starting with Nixon—have been doing all they can to give the DEA the power to try and put an end to the drugs coming into the country. We shut down the Okeechobee mess and arrested twenty-nine people. Nine of those were longtime residents of the area. It's the money. People just figure it's worth the risk."

"It's like Tito Ramirez. The money was all he thought about. I'll call the DA and see what we can do to protect him. Although with Santos dead, there will be no Grand Jury trial," Gabe said. "With no Grand Jury trial, Nora won't have to testify. Thank God for that."

"Right you are, my friend," Dan stood and walked to the door. "I'll stop by tomorrow before we take off."

"You need a ride to Tampa?" Gabe asked.

"O'Donnell hired a van," Dan told him. "Besides, you have to spend some time with Nora." He started to walk down the hall and did a quick about turn. "By the way, I make a great best man," he said smiling and chuckling as he walked away.

EPILOGUE

Twilight was settling over the little church in the grove as bats swooped overhead. The wooden structure was spilling over with friends and workers. The March orange blossoms filled the air with their sweet sent. Father Miguel wore his best cassock and vestments for the wedding of Sheriff Gabriel McAlister and Nora Ann Hollister.

Gabe stood nervously waiting, twisting his Stetson in his hands, beside his best man Dan Parker. He had Dan double and triple check the rings in his pockets. They were dressed in dark suits, white shirts and bolo ties. Rosita had stuck a sprig of orange blossom in their lapels—crying all the time.

When Nora appeared in the back of the church with her grandfather, guitars and a violin struck up the wedding march.

Gabe watched as the most beautiful woman he had ever seen walked down the aisle to become his wife. Nora wore her mother's wedding gown and a wreath of orange blossoms in her hair.

"You'd better be good to her," Gramps whispered to Gabe as he handed him his only grandchild.

"I will. She carries a gun," Gabe whispered back.

Gramps went to his seat beside Rosita and Hector. Rosita was wiping tears of joy from her eyes. Rex, fresh and clean from a bath, laid his head upon Gramps' knee. Gabe's parents and his sister and her family sat in the next row.

The vows were said and the rings exchanged. Father Miguel said, "You may now kiss the bride," and the gathering erupted in shouts and cheers.

Gabe and Nora walked hand-in-hand to receive the well wishes of everyone and the start of a grand fiesta. Lights twinkled in the trees, and music flowed. Tables were loaded down with every conceivable dish.

Finding a quiet table, the newlyweds reached across the table to hold hands. They looked out over the people they had come to love.

"You know, Mrs. McAlister . . ."
"Yeah, I know Mr. McAllister . . ."

They both knew that there was nothing better than being with friends and family enjoying themselves in the Florida orange groves.

Acknowledgements

I wish to thank all my author friends down here in Florida. They are so supportive and encouraging.

I also want to thank the DEA agent in Washington D.C. that took the time to talk to me and answer some of my questions about the Medellin Cartel in Florida in the 1980's.

The Florida Orange Growers Association provide me with information on how the oranges are picked and about the migrant population that works the groves.

Sadly, the groves are disappearing and houses are taking their place. Rural Florida, the groves and ranches will not be there for future generations.

More books by Brenda M. Spalding

The Green Lady Inn series
Broken Branches
Whispers in time
Hidden assets
The Spell box

Award winning
Bottle Alley
Honey Tree Farm – For the Love of the
Beekeeper's Daughter

For the children

The Hayden series
Just Batty
Hayden's Garden
Hayden's Halloween
Hayden and the Honey Farm
Collections
Hayden's Adventures on the Farm

Princess Annie and the Unicorn
Where's Teddy
Coming fall 2017
Sailing Away to Nod

Author Brenda M. Spalding grew up in Newton Massachusetts. After traveling with her military husband for twenty-two years she settled Bradenton, Florida. She has a son, daughter and a grandson in the area.
She started her writing career in 2012 publishing her first children's book. In 2012. She was a co-founder of ABC Books 4 Children & Adults, Inc. She member of the National League of American Pen women, The Saras authors connection, Gulf Coast Sisters in Crime and the Florida Writ Association.

www.ingramcontent.com/pod-product-compliance
Lightning Source LLC
Chambersburg PA
CBHW071523110726

47908CB00003B/927